ISBN-13:
978-1499548419

ISBN-10:
1499548419

Written and produced in Jamaica by Clive Myrie

PREFACE

Sitting in the community of Red Berry one late evening talking with
a number of old folks including my cousin and feeling the secret
therapeutic effects of the deep rural atmosphere, I was thrilled. We
were at a stand pipe just in front of the Seventh Day Adventist
church. The snow white tombs on the church property prompted a
discussion on ghost/duppy, which I found very stimulating. I said to
myself that these wonderful stories cannot remain a deep rural
secret; the world had to know about it. The idea of the book was
born......

FOREWORD

Anyone who knows Clive Myrie automatically ascribes the words: creative, inventive and innovative to his character. It was therefore no surprise when he indicated that after a brief discussion with some acquaintances, he had an idea for a story which he thought everyone who loved a good suspense story should get a chance to enjoy. A few weeks later**, *'The Unrested Spirit'*** was birthed.

You will want to put the story down, but can't. The journey, however, has just begun.

ACKNOWLEDGEMENT:

I would like the following people:
The people of Red Berry district who were the catalyst for the writing of the book
My wife and family for their encouragement and support
Meleisa Witter- For her technical assistance and for the editing, proof-reading and other fine tuning she added to the book. For all the advice and encouragement she imparted

THE UNRESTED SPIRIT

BY CLIVE MYRIE

Red Berry is a quiet district situated just outside the town of Porus in the parish of Manchester. The district is almost at the eastern end of the parish and about thirty minutes from the parish capital. Red Berry is quite typical of a deep rural district, with poor housing structures, for the most part, and a shortage of essential infrastructure and social amenities.

The population is small, having just a few hundred inhabitants with the average age being approximately fifty. There is an almost even gender mix, however, there is an obvious age disparity with a near void between the very young and the very old. Majority of the population are Christians who attend the Seventh Day Adventist church in the district. There are pockets of Rastafarians and people with unattached faith. None of the Christians in the district were strict adherents to the principles of the Sabbath including the Pastor and the Deacons.

It's a predominantly farming district though a small number of the residents engage in charcoal production. Subsistence farming though, seems to be the order of the day. Banana, yam, breadfruit, pumpkin, sweet potatoes, and cassava are the main staples while oranges, grapefruit, ackee, naseberry and sugar cane are the main fruits trees grown. There are a few poultry and cattle farmers, with a handful engaged in piggery and goat rearing. These livestock farmers are usually more commercially inclined in their business activities

Each residential house is meters apart, and is unfenced in most cases. Many of the yards are burial sites for the family members of many generations.

These tombs, are in many cases, are well preserved with regular cleaning and weeding. There is a fresh coat of paint which is applied annually during a special event called Tombing. At Tombing, family members and friends meet at the sight of the tomb, where the painting is done. A grand feast of food and music follows.

At nights, majority of the district is so dark that catching sight of someone a mere foot away is impossible. The vegetation in the district is lush and untamed and tends to dominates most of the physical structures on the landscape. There are no clearly defined roadways, but instead dirt tracks which are narrowed by prolific vegetation growth. There is however, the main one that leads into the district which is paved up to the first two hundred metres or so. It is the only vehicular entrance and exit thoroughfare inside the district.

For entertainment, there is one main shop in the district with light and music that attracts its patrons. Most of the males and a few females will drink rum and other alcoholic beverages while engaging in a game of domino or bingo. These games go on for hours even after the proprietor has shut his/her door for business. This happens almost every week night and is a surety on the weekends. Sometimes there is a pre-planned open air church service at a designated open lot, while there are the occasional nine nights and sound system dances and parties.

The residents are usually kind, jovial and express a happy demeanour. They always appear to be free of life's stresses, an attribute which I think is directly related to their simplistic lifestyle coupled with the motto; "Jamaica no problem"
Fredrick Grashan (aka Freddy) and Malito James (aka Mally) are two of the senior statesmen of the district. Both are highly respected as clergymen and farmers in the area. Freddy is married for over thirty years with his wife Maria Grashan six children and several grand and great grandchildren.
Freddy lives alone with his wife and two of his great grand children Matthew and Mavis, with the rest of the family migrated to other parishes. Matthew is seven years old and his sister Mavis, five years old. They both attend the Red Berry Primary and Infant School which is situated inside the district, just walking distance from their home.

Freddy is about 1.2 metres in height and is of slim build. Although he has just celebrated his seventy fifth birthday, youthful facial wan and his agility makes him appear much younger. Freddy is soft spoken. But still commands the respect of all and sundry in the district. He is the pastor at the Red Berry SDA and is considered a district leader. Freddy is the person most people would confide in. He would offer counseling to members of the district free of cost and would often intervene in family and other domestic disputes in the district.

Freddy's wife Maria is a Deacon at the same church. She is also a farmer and a devoted housewife.

Mally with his wife Angella live in his two bedroom board house. Unlike Freddy, Mally is short, stoutly built and loud mouthed He is sixty nine years old and clean shaved. Mally produce charcoal for a living. His two children who were raised in the same house are now deceased. Both died tragically in a motor vehicle accident while on their way from school many years ago.

This incident has devastated the James family to this day. Mally and Angella's involvement in the church as a Deacons has provided the only solace for them after the incident. Angella thinks that Mally was too much of a strict father and that his actions may have led to his children's demise.

Angella often recalls that tragic day; on the morning before the children left for school, they were violently flogged by Mally for not cleaning their shoe the night before.

The dereliction of basic household chores and decorum were met with the physical might of Mally.

While the kids are being punished, Angella had to watch in pity. Both Eric and Erica often expressed the desire to run away from home.

The burning desires were always quelled by Angella's plea. Angella thinks the children, who should have been home earlier, deliberately delayed to avoid getting home too early.

Angella's shared her son's desire to become a soldier after graduation. Eric had already developed the physical attributes to make him a good soldier.

He was 1.8 meters tall and medium built and evinced great athletic abilities. Erica was more like her mom soft spoken and submissive. Both Eric and Erica had a fervent love for reggae music and would sing and dance to their favourite tunes playing on the radio; in the absence of Mally of course.

The tombs of Mally's children, Eric and Erica are situated at the front of the yard and is grilled all the way around. Both tombs are painted in a bright white colour, which is difficult to look at in the glowing midday sun. On the headstone of each tomb are the words written boldly in black.

GONE TOO SOON, MAY YOUR SOUL REST IN PEACE...

At the side of Eric's tomb, inside the grilled enclosure is a thorny tree known in Jamaica as Kasha which seems to have become a permanent fixture there. No matter how often the area is de-bushed, that particular Kasha seems to reappear in a few days and grows rapidly to a height of 1.8 meters then seem to go into a growth suspension mode.

The Kasha is noticeably green all year round even when other trees in the yard showed signs of stress from the prolonged drought. Another significant feature of the tree was that the thorns are two and a half times that of the typical kasha tree.

Mally was the only one who paid any keen interest in these observations and promptly dismissed it as another freak of nature.

It is now the 30th June 1999, one week before the annual tombing event at the James's resident, and activities picked up in earnest. Mally, Fredrick and some other members of the district start a massive clean-up campaign. Usually, the yard and the track leading thereto would be de-bushed.

The cooking area would be clearly defined. The spots for the tents and the seating, the parking area for cars and the lighting fixtures would all be defined and prepared. All the labour and most of the food contributions would be a voluntary exercise; this is the traditional spirit across rural Jamaica.

Ken Kennedy aka Mass Ken who lives about three hundred meters from the James' family, is a poultry farmer and a great district figure. Mass Ken has two sons, Kenneth and Kenny Kennedy ages 23 years old and 25 years old respectively.

Both sons assist their father in the chicken business, both in the area of production and marketing. Kenny takes pleasure in beating on his younger brother Kenneth asserting himself has his boss in the business.

They have had many clashes in the past with Kenny having a one hundred percent win record. Kenneth quite cognizant of his physical limitations accepts the subservient role respectfully. Mass Ken's wife Kerona Kennedy, is a stay home mom who takes care of all household chores. Mass Ken had promised Mally and Angella twelve mature chickens for the event, three more than what he contributed last year.

Mass Ken and his boys would kill and prepare the chickens for the cook. Mr Danny Peart (aka Dan) lives in the adjoining district is the known master chef. He prepares the food at all major events in and around the district.

Dan operates a jerk chicken/pork business out in the town of Porus and gets great patronage for his handy work. Dan has volunteered his service for the event. Mass Ballack, the cattle farmer has offered a Ram Goat and a Bull.

Other members of the district pledged their support offering ground provision, rice, flour, spices and condiments and everything that would result in a grand feast.

On the day of the Tombing, everything was in place and moving smoothly. Pots on fire; drink on ice; music box warming up and people started to gather around. A young couple from the district John and Denise got into a small fracas near the Tomb in the James's yard.

This was quickly squashed by some members of the district. John is an abusive policeman who is stationed at the Mandeville police station. His violent and abusive reputation precedes him anywhere he goes. Later, Mally and Angella beckons to the sound system operator to stop the music and proceeded to take the microphone. Mally then takes the microphone; "A pleasant evening to you all and welcome to another of our Tombing which represents the anniversary of the death of our children.

At this time I want to call on Pastor Fredrick Grashan to bless the gathering" Freddy stepped forward and delivered a beautiful prayer which lasted several minutes. Angella then takes the microphone from Freddy and proceeds to bless the food. After the prayer Angella led the gathering into a plethora of gospel songs, this in keeping with the traditions of the Tombing ceremony.

By this time, the gathering swelled to well over one hundred people from within and outside the district. Freddy and Mally reached for a one litre bottle of over-proof white rum and proceed to sprinkle around the yard while the crowd sang. The sprinkling of the rum is believed to rid the yard of all evil spirits.

By now, the function was in high gear, the music has restarted, and most people by now were drinking and eating.

People formed separate groups and engaged in conversations, domino and card games while others just stand and observe.

One could not help but notice John physically and verbally abusing his girlfriend Denise Boland.

He was obviously show-boating while two of his colleagues from the station looked on from close proximity.

Corporal Donovan, a close friend of John and Denise came over to the couple and tried to lighten the tension between

John and Denise. John was having rum and coke like most of the people in the gathering, and was downing his third glass. On one occasion, while pulling on Denise, some of his drink spilled over onto the Kasha tree which was inside the grill partitioning the tomb. Denise noticed that the tree shook rapidly for a couple of seconds. "Did you see that?" Denise asked John. "See what?" John asked in reply.

Denise described the shaking action of the tree to John who began to taunt her about seeing things. Denise, in trying to get confirmation of her sighting, proceeded to ask others in close proximity to the event if they saw what had happened.

To her dismay and annoyance, no one else saw what had happened. She however noticed a frightful look on Donovan's face as if he had just seen a ghost. In her now frantic quest to get some sort of alliance, she insisted, almost begging, Donovan to confirm her sighting. Donovan, without uttering another word, walked away and rejoined his other colleagues.

Denise looked across to Donovan who was standing some distance away, and noticed the obvious change in his demeanour. He was no longer active in his group's discussions and he repeatedly looked in her direction, only to turn away his face each time their eyes made contact.

Denise Boland is a teacher at the Red Berry Primary and Infant school. She is also the church secretary, the head of the 4H movement in the division and the vice president of the Red Berry Citizen's Association. She is most times quiet and unassuming and wears a permanent smile which is not to be mistaken for weakness. She often demonstrates a firm resolve which she uses as a tool to keep the, most often unruly children, in check.

This characteristic is in striking contrast to the submissive disposition she exhibits around John. Denise is tall, approximately 1.5 metres tall and slender. She has fair complexion and jet black natural hair.

She doesn't wear jewelry or make-up and is as natural as they come. Denise, like all the other professionals are well respected inside the district. She is an avid church attendee but is confused about her faith, or maybe she is too open minded.

Denise has one very close friend Sheila which is surprising, based on her many social and civic affiliations. It may be as a result of her dual dispositions. Denise doesn't confide in anyone that easily, and although not antisocial, she seldom shares or discusses her personal business with others.

Denise lives in a three bedroom house with her mother Gloria Boland and her father Godfrey Boland. Gloria is the district dressmaker and like her daughter, she holds a prominent position in the church where she has served as the treasurer for the past six years. Godfrey on the other hand is a jack of all trades. He, however, specializes in cabinet making. Both Godfrey and Gloria operate their business from home. Godfrey works from a small room which is an extension of the main building and situated at the rear of it. A section of the spacious living room is partitioned by curtains to facilitate Gloria's operation.

Sheila is quiet and unassuming and like Denise, she is a Christian, however, she doesn't hold a position at the church. Sheila is unemployed at this time as she recently lost her job as a sales clerk at Wholesale Variety Store in the town of Mandeville. Both Sheila and Denise were classmates at the Porus High School. Denise continued her studies at the Teacher's College in Mandeville, while Sheila went straight into the working world. Her first and only job was at the Wholesale Variety Store.

Sheila is a great hair stylist, who is constantly urged by Denise to pursue courses in Cosmetology to certify her skill. Sheila lives next door with her Aunt whom she despises.

She spends most of her time with the Bolands who always welcome her with open arms.

She is highly industrious and would make a perfect housekeeper. She is a "clean freak" who doesn't have to be invited to perform a domestic task. The Bolands have often compensated her with a small but greatly appreciated stipend.

Nightfall has descended rapidly, and a sudden shower of rain poured down on the proceedings and forced the gathering under the tents. The rain was quite heavy and lasted for nearly an hour. People had begun to disperse. Denise had to take a shortcut through the woodlands because the main road to her home was inundated by the heavy showers.

Both John and Denise bid their friends farewell and began their trek home which is a fairly short distance from the James's house when using the shortcut. John took home Denise and started his return trip to the James's home.

While walking through the woodland John began to encounter some difficulties as it seemed as though the Kasha trees along the path came alive. Then John began shivering as he noticed a sudden drop in temperature. He tried moving but was but was rendered motionless and speechless and seemed to be having a grand mal seizure. The trees were swinging and shaking violently as they surrounded John. They pierced John all over his body with a fatal one to his heart.

No one heard John's cry for help as the event unfolded so quickly. After the act, the trees resumed their original position as they rid themselves of any bloody evidence.

The following morning Denise received a call from one of John's colleagues at the Mandeville police station enquiring the whereabouts of John. "I have no idea, he followed me home, saw me safely inside then left" she nervously replied; sensing something may be wrong. After getting off the phone with the police, Denise dialed John's mobile only to get voice mail.

She called his parents and friends but no one knew his whereabouts. Come mid day, and still no sign of John who should have been at work since eight o'clock that morning. Denise's mind was in a quandary as she sat at home awaiting a call from John.

Later that same day, Mass Ballack when into the woodland to round up his cattle as part of his daily routine, when he stumbled upon the body. The body was lying face down in a pool of blood. The garments on the body was tattered and a cellular phone lay beside the body.

Frightened, and rendered speechless by shock, Mass Ballack ran none stop to the James's home where other members of the district was still there assisting in the cleaning up of the yard. Finally, breathing heavily, he recovered a little. "Dead man in bush" was all he could utter.

A group of people quickly went into the direction where Mass Ballack pointed. They too stumbled upon the gruesome sight. Word spread quickly, and in a few minutes a large gathering of people from the district along with the police were on the scene. On discovering that the body was that of their missing college, the inspector sent a team of police to inform the deceased parent, next of kin and his girlfriend.

The scene was processed by a team of investigators and forensic officers who arrived at the scene quickly. Doctor Harry Reynold, the Chief Medical Officer employed to the Mandeville Public hospital was there to confirm and pronounce the victim dead. The body was later removed to the morgue.

The entire district was in shock, as this kind of event is a rarity in this neck of the woods. Prima facie, it would appear as if the victim had been stabbed multiple times all over the body by an assailant using an ice pick or other similar device. It was now six o'clock in the evening and the investigation had started in earnest. The investigating officer ordered a team to take in Denise for questioning, however, on hearing the news, Denise was already on her way to the station crying uncontrollably.

All the team members at the station were in a sombre mood. By this time, most of John's family members were at the station seeking answers. Denise arrived and immediately became subjected to interrogation by the investigators.

Denise was subsequently released after her interrogation. She went over and grieved with the other family members. In the meanwhile the Police remained on patrol conducting a thorough search of the area

An unofficial bulletin was out, cautioning members of the district to be on the lookout for anyone acting suspiciously. The media were present in the district conducting interviews and gathering reports. The following day, some of John's colleagues along with his parents and Denise started to make plans for the "Dead Yard,"

Now, *in Jamaica, a "Dead Yard" is the former home of someone who has recently died and has not been buried as yet. The "dead yard' is actually the nightly gathering of members of the district and other guests who will visit and bring support for the bereaved family while they prepare for the funeral. Tents will be erected and seating will be provided for the guests. The host is expected to provide refreshment usually soup; tea, coffee and alcohol (mainly white rum). Dominoes and card game will be features of the entertainment package along with prayers and the singing of religious songs. All this will culminate at the Wake.*
As is customary, the residents trump up their cash and kind to give support to the family. The constabulary force has pledged to cover the funeral expense for the family and to contribute to the Dead Yard activities.

Day two after the incident, and there is still no breakthrough in the case. The autopsy revealed that the victim died from punctured left aorta which resulted in a cardiac arrest. The body, according to report had over two hundred puncture wounds. It is also speculated that these wounds came from a sharp metal object. The forensic report showed two sets of footprint going in one direction but only one set (that of the victim) going in the other direction.

This scenario puzzled the investigators while at the same time assisted in extricating Denise as a potential suspect. The intricacy of the case is compounded by the fact that there are no eyewitnesses, and no weapon(s).

Another day was again coming to an end, and the dead yard was buzzing with activities. Domino games were the main entertainment featured along with some card games. A group of elders from the church were praying with the family indoor. Some of the other attendants were just hanging around in groups discussing various issues.
The police were present in their numbers, assuring the residents of their safety. The patrol by the police throughout the district was ongoing. The security men, while promoting safety, tried their uttermost best not to disrupt the normal lives of the residents. They did not restrict the movements of the residents within the district.

However the police were everywhere in sight and that was sufficient to allay the fear of the residents. Four days went by with no arrest by the police. Several theories were examined by the investigators, but none seemed to be seamless. The incident tops all discussions in the district and the media for days.
The district is very fearful at this time and the finger pointing and speculation had already begun.
One week after the incident, the only form of nightly entertainment was the Dead Yard.

The shops in the district had to be closed earlier as the Dead Yard became the preferred choice. The regularly scheduled open air prayer meetings were now being held at the Dead Yard.

Even with the very strong police detachment in the district there were still some residents who were apprehensive and scared to venture too far from their homes, especially at nights. However, this was the case for only a small number of residents.

Saturday came; a very busy day at the shop. Only a Wake or a huge district party can attract the regular die hard patrons away from Saturday night at the main shop. The main shop (the Blue Shop) is owned by the Alexander's family and has served the district for many years. The Blue Shop has two sections, separated internally by a dry wall with a common door between both sections. There is a grocery shop on the left side in relation to the front door.

The grocery section is run by Mrs Alexander for the most part. The other section is a well spacious Pub which is furnished with high stools along with a few portable plastic tables and chairs. A well polished ceramic top board counter serves as a line of demarcation, separating the area of pleasure from the area of commerce.

The pub is extended at the front by making the shape of the number seven from an aerial perspective. The area is well lit with bright fluorescence bulbs all around. The Pub however, is illuminated by a deep blue light with wonderful and compelling radiance, which may be one of the main attractive forces for pulling so many patrons.

The drinking and gaming activities usually start at about six o'clock and goes on up to midnight and beyond. As the patrons gather and activities heighten, Mr Black (aka Bigga) comes in. His loud mouth is always heard before he is seen. Bigga resides in the adjoining district where he is known as the district bully.

His towering structure is imposing and when combined with his loud mouth, tends to drive fear in people. Bigga is a wife beater and was once incarcerated for physically abusing his teenage son. When Bigga arrived at the shop, he immediately states that he will be sitting around the domino table next, regardless of those before him. The compliance was acknowledged by the silence and lack of response from anyone there.

Then comes Mr Max Archer. He is one of the most affluent persons living in the parish. Mr Archer grew up in Red Berry, but migrated with his family to the USA when he was only a teen. He is now a retired engineer and a successful family man. Whenever he comes around, you can expect the rum, beer and other drinks to flow endlessly.

Mr Archer stepped up to the shop door and immediately became the focal point. They surrounded him like iron filings around a magnet and greeted him like a king. Mr Archer did not disappoint. He opened the bar to his friends and they drank with reckless abandon, bottle after bottle and glass after glass.

After midnight the shop was closed and most of the patrons had left for home. Bigga was the last to leave as he struggled from one point to the next. Highly intoxicated, Bigga was lying on the pavement next to the shop and everyone left him there. He finally awoke after a couple of hours and started the lonely trek home. Having slept off the deep haziness of the liquor, even though he was still a bit foggy, he was quite aware of his surrounding and his compass was in good order.

As he walked along the roadside, he felt a sudden drop in temperature when passing the James's home. It got so cold that he tried running but realized he was not moving.

He tried calling for help, however there were no sound coming from his usually loud mouth.

He started to experience the head swelling effect, while he was held stationary in a spiritual gridlock. While still aware, but helpless he noticed the Kasha tree from the James's yard come alive and float towards him. He stood there helpless as the spirit punctured his body hundreds of time removing his eye ball in the process and inflicting fatal wounds.

The tree was returned to its' original position with no evidence of blood stains. Bigga succumbed to his injuries and his lifeless body, wrapped in now, tattered blood stained clothes lay in the middle of the road in front of Mally's home.

At daylight, Mally who is an early riser opened his door and was shocked at what he saw, he was so fright filled, that he stood frozen on his verandah for minutes with his eyes pulping out of his socket and his heart beat thumping out of control.

Mally finally overcame the initial shock and started shouting his wife's name trying to wake her up. In her half sleepy state she barely answered.

Mally kept on shouting her name until he finally got her full attention. Angella, now fully awake, walked to the verandah where Mally was standing.

With his eyes still affixed on the gruesome image, Mally pointed to the body. Both Angella and Mally went into immediate speech arrest.

With tears of fright and sorrow running down her eyes and her now shaking knees incapable of supporting her body weight, she dropped heavily on one of the verandah chairs.

Mally nervously, whispered a prayer seeking divine strength, which was promptly granted. Mally was able to extricate himself from the grip of shock and went to sit beside Angella offering words of consolation.

Mally then, gathers himself, went inside where he picked up the mobile phone and return beside his wife.

Mally made his first call to his best friend and church colleague Freddy. Mally then called Patrick who is a policeman and a close friend of the family.

News in these rural communities spread rapidly and soon the scene in front of the James's home was over flooded with curious onlookers.

A week and a day and another death which bears striking resemblance to the first have spun the district once again into a bowl of fear.

The speculations were raging. The large gathering was fragmented into several pockets of people each submitting their own views, their own fears and revealing their own expressions of emotion.

Some were seen in a group cuddle trying to console each other. Some were weeping openly. Others were speechless and one could hear some discussing jungle justice.

Leading that call for vigilante justice was Mass Ballack who uttered "we can't allow our citizens to be slaughtered like dogs while the police seem helpless to protect us. We will find the perpetrator and hand over his head to the police" He further called for support from other members of the district. Within minutes of Mass Ballack's announcement, the team of vigilante has swollen to well over thirty members (mostly male) and growing.

By this time the scene was awash with police and media personnel from all the major media centres in Jamaica. Police teams from Kingston, Mandeville and Clarendon bearing ranks from Corporal to Superintendent were combing the scene, looking for clues. Interviews from the police investigators and the media reporters were on in earnest. The hearse arrived with the undertakers, but had to wait for the arrival of Dr. Harry Reynold. Doctor Reynolds arrived several minutes later and performed his routine. The body was then removed to the morgue.

The investigators, in trying to retrace the course of events, visited the corner shop where Bigga was last seen by friends. The investigators started by interviewing Mr and Mrs Alexander. The team of investigators requested the names of all the patrons who were playing dominoes and other games on the night when Bigga was last seen alive. The investigation was thorough.

As a rule, *policing most deep rural communities in Jamaica is quite an easy task, as the residents there are usually honest in their compliance. This is true however, only under normal circumstances.*

Meanwhile, Mass Ballack's team of vigilante was already discussing critical strategies in their effort to dispense their own jungle justice to the person(s) involved in these two atrocities. One of their main strategies is to take turn to keep a watch on the district, especially at night. Denise who is still grieving from Johns' tragedy urged the group to exact revenge for her boyfriend's murder.

Hours have elapsed, and the investigations continue. The Police Superintendent for the zone called for an emergency meeting with the district members at the Red Berry Seventh Day Adventist church for five o'clock later that afternoon.
It was now one full hour before the commencement of the emergency meeting and Denise along with Freddy and his wife are all grouped up inside Mally's yard leaning backwards on the grill which borders the Tombs and watching the hearse as it arrives on the scene.
The air was still, the sun was out and there was a sudden hush around which plunged the place into silence for over a minute. The silence was broken by the closing of the hearse door.
Mally joined Denise and the Grashans as they all watched the proceedings. Out of the corner of an eye, Denise saw the Kasha tree shiver momentarily. She then looked around immediately at the tree and saw the thorns retracting to its' original position.
Denise looked at Mally in a curious but quizzical way which prompted a "what?" from him." Nothing" said Denise who leaned off the grill and stood in front of the rest of the group facing the Kasha tree.
In order to protect the scrutiny of her own sanity, Denise kept her sightings to herself. With her eyes dead fixed on the Kasha tree and unconcerned with the rest of the discussion, the attention was now on her. Freddy asked Denise if she was feeling ok. And with a delayed response eyes still affixed to the tree, she responded "yes I am" It was time for the meeting, so they all dispersed and headed towards the church.

The meeting commenced on time and was cheered by the Superintendent. The meeting was well attended and the church was bursting at the seams. "We from this police division promise to bring the perpetrator(s) to justice. These two horrific crimes which have happened within days have covered the entire district with a blanket of fear. We, the police, are however imploring your fullest support in helping us to solve these crimes.

We want to offer our deepest condolences to the families and friends of the victims. We owe it to you and the rest of the district to apprehend the suspect(s) hand over the suspect(s) to the criminal court so that justice can prevail. I also want to personally warn against jungle justice.

I know, as a district, you're all hurting now, however I insist that the law should run its' course. Taking the matter in your own hands is a crime which is punishable under the law." Murmurs of dissent were heard coming from the gathering. As the grumblers became more vociferous, the Superintendent had to intervene and demanded silence.

"I will seek permission from my commissioner to establish a temporary police post in the area until we can catch the culprit(s) and restore normalcy inside the district" This assertion was met with applause of acceptance. "Furthermore," he said, "I want you the residents of this district and to take all the possible precautions to protect yourself.

I want you to walk in groups, avoid walking on the road at nights, keep your eyes and ears open and be your brothers' keeper." In closing, the Superintendent reminds the citizens of the stations' telephone number and promised to increase patrol in the area for as long as it takes to solve the "murder" cases. The Superintendent was greeted with handshakes all around.

Only a few residents from Red Berry bother to venture outside the district to attend Bigga's Dead Yard. The few who make the trek, travelled in numbers and visit very infrequently. There were many good reasons for this. As a bully, Bigga was not well liked, additionally; the Red Berry district already had an active dead yard to support in their own community.

Three weeks have now passed since the death of John and still there was no breakthrough in his case of Bigga's. Both cases have now attracted some of the finest investigators and forensic scientists on the island. The autopsy reports for both bodies are identical.

The number of puncture wounds to the body is the same; the orientations of the wounds differ in some places. In both cases there seemed to be a minimal struggle by the victims which further complicate the case.

Both victims were strong and possessed great physical and athletic abilities, and so it's the thinking of the investigating officers that it would take several strong men to subdue and render both men motionless. Finger prints on both bodies along with DNA evidence did not support this theory.

Also the lack of the attacker(s) footprint in the case of John has compounded the problem even greater. The investigators were into the district daily, trying to find clues to aid in their ongoing investigations.

The Superintendent got the approval of the commissioner to set up a temporary police post in the area much to the delight of the residents. A forty foot steel container, already retro-fitted was transported and placed into one of the open lots, in close proximity to the woodlands where John's body was found.

The post was manned by a rotatable six man crew with Sergeant Webber in charge. Sergeant Webber hails from the parish of Kingston in a volatile district called Tower Hill.

He grew up on the streets and learned the way of war and hostilities early in his life. He learned to survive on bare essentials as he was orphaned at the age of five when both parents and his older sibling were gunned down in the area. Webber was cornered and held by a policeman (now deceased) during a shootout in the district. It was alleged that Webber and friends held up and robbed a delivery goods truck on the main street just outside the district.

The police was alerted and quickly responded, a shootout ensued, Webber was the only survivor. Sergeant Webber, has always recalled that story with Corporal Donovan, telling him that the police who accosted him pointed the gun at him and said in a surprisingly soft tone, "I can kill you but I won't, I am gonna spare your life, so make good use of it" Webber in recounting the incident, said the police walked away without arresting him.

The same policeman, he recalled, visited the district the following day saw him on the road and called him. Webber said the policeman enquired about his family, his place of dwelling and his schooling among other things. The policeman he said was successful in getting him into a Boys home where he was fed, sheltered, and schooled.
He also said his interest in the police force was a direct influence of that police. He recalled sadly that the police was killed by a gunman's bullet shortly after he joined the force. The policeman's death only served to increase the anger and strong antipathy of Mr Webber.

Sergeant Webber is known as a no-nonsense crime fighting cop who have had close brushes with the law as it related to human rights abuses. Some people think he is mean spirited, and that having him there would defeat the purpose of having the post there in the first place. Some say he is a great crime fighter, but lacks the people skill necessary to be involved with district policing.

Whatever some may say about the sergeant, many still feel safer with him at the helm. The post was equipped with a radio service car and three motorcycles to aid in mobility and a radio communication system. A perimeter chain-link fence was erected around the container and security lights posted at the four corners of the premises.

A very visible semi-circular metal sign painted in blue and have the words RED BERRY POLICE POST written in white. In the mind of many of the residents, this structure represents something monumental in such a remote district and created a sense of pride and achievement; even though the district was relatively crime free before the couple of recent incidents.

Sergeant Webber wasted no time in asserting himself as the new district boss. He held a meeting with some of the residents at the Alexander's shop where he imposed a few changes much to the dislike and disgust of many who were present; Sergeant Webber said "I am here to clean up this district of all rogue elements and undesirables. There will be no dances or parties in the area going on beyond 6pm"

He also stated that all planned events and functions must first get his approval. Addressing Mr Alexander; 'I notice that your shop does not have a permit to sell alcohol and other spirits if you do" he added, " it should be clearly advertised on the wall for all to see; "It is my intention to apply for a permit" said Mr Alexander, " well I will have to close down that section of your business until you are in compliance with the law of the land" this was met with a chants of anger from the small gathering, who were regular patrons.

"We don't want people like you in our district" exclaimed one angry protester. The Sergeant walked over to him grabbed him by the waist of his pant proceeded to threaten him verbally. By this time, the vociferous crowd protested the Sergeant's action with chants of boos and treats to report his action to the Superintendent. The abused resident was subsequently released and the Sergeant left for his post. The action of the Sergeant spread an air of resentment across the district.

That very same day, some of the residents met with Pastor Freddy Grashan to complain about the actions of the Sergeant. Freddy promised to have words with Sergeant Webber the following day. The meeting took place as promised the next day at the police post and Pastor Freddy tried to get Sergeant Webber to make some compromises on some of the rules he laid down the day before. However, all the talk proved futile. Sergeant Webber could be a very hard nut to crack and hardly anyone can get him to change his stance once he establishes one.

John's funeral is scheduled to be held in a couple of days and the traditional Nine Night (Wake) is slated for the day before. A Wake in rural Jamaica is like a grand farewell event which takes on a party setting and church setting in one. Unlike Wakes in other parts of the world where the body of the dead is present, the Jamaican wake has no such thing. In many cases the host hires a musical band which is directed by a DJ (a person holding the microphone and chanting musical lyrics).

This ceremony takes place in the open yard; sometimes a large tent is erected. There is usually a small table situated in the centre of the tent. The table usually has placed on it, a bible and a bottle of rum. The chanter will read verses from the bible as the gathering listen attentively. The rum is a significant ritualistic tool in the life of the rural folks. It is believed to ward off evil spirits while at the same time offering protection from same.

The rum is the most popularly consumed beverage at any Jamaican Wake. It is also sprinkled around the yard where the wake is being held for protection. It is also customary for one to release a few drops from their drink of rum on the ground before drinking as a mark of respect for the dead.

People in these parts of the country look forward to these events for entertainment reasons and for commerce. Once a wake is in full swing, there will be people singing and dancing nonstop.

Vendors would set up their booths with liquor and snacks on the outside of the yard to try and cash in on this rare moment of commerce.

Smoke from drums of the few "Jerk/BBQ Vendors" would be seen floating in the air. The atmosphere is festive and everyone is in a jolly mood; even the family of the deceased. Dress code is thrown through the window as it varies from very skimpy erotic shorts to a "ground sweeping" dress.

Any attempt to prevent a Wake from being held will certainly be met with violence actions.

Sighting a possible disastrous outcome, Pastor Grashan take it upon himself to pay the Superintendent a visit by the police station in Mandeville. Here Mr Greshan seeks an official permission from the Superintendent to have the function hosted by the family. Pastor Grashan took the time to complain about Sergeant Webber's behaviour among other things.

The Superintendent calls Sergeant Webber to confirm his granting of the Wake in the area and spoke to him about some of his actions as reported by the pastor. Freddy expressed his gratitude to the Superintendent then departs the office, but not before a firm handshake was affected. On his way back to the district, Freddy was sure he is now firmly placed in Sergeant's bad book for reporting him to his superior officer.

In the meantime, back in the district, the anger of the two deaths is now superseded by the anger brought on by Sergeant Webber and his imposition of some stringent rules. His actions have impacted negatively on the spirit of the district.

Their culture was now threatened and the Sergeant has now become the villain in the eye of many of the residents. The tension heightened as the date of the Wake gets nearer. No one apart from Pastor Freddy and Sergeant knows that permission is granted.

When Freddy returned to the district, all the fears were allayed as the news of the permission spread rapidly. Preparation for the Wake began in earnest. And in keeping with tradition and the spirit of the district, donations for the event came from all quarters of the district, and like the Tombing events several weeks ago, everything fell in place very quickly.

At Denise's house, she was a nervous wreck. For the past week, she has been having the same dreams night after night. She keeps on visioning the Kasha tree at the James's house comes alive and taking on human form.

The tree then commands the other Kasha trees to come alive by just by a simple limb waving gesture.

She dreams that the Kasha all have the ability to extend and harden their thorns.

She felt ridiculous to even mention these dreams to anyone. Even the two previous experiences she had with the Kasha tree at the James's resident, she labeled as just an imagination inflicted by emotional stresses brought on by the two incidents.

Angella is thirty two years old and lives with her mom and dad. She has no siblings, but she is never lonely as her best friend and next door neighbour Sheila is always around her at home. Though the two are very close, they don't reveal everything to each other.

There was an obvious change in Denise's disposition which didn't go unnoticed. "Something is not right with you" uttered Sheila. "I'm fine" replied Denise. "No you're not, wanna tell me what's going on?" Sheila asks. I said I was ok" Denise insisted. "Ok, if you say so" Sheila murmured sarcastically.

Thursday arrives and it is a couple of hours before the Wake gets into full swing. People start to gather around in numbers. The tents were already erected, the band was in place, and the pots are on fire and the liquor on ice.

The vendors have started to take their position in front the yard. The band begins to warm up, the chanter testing the microphone, the seating capacity now full.

Very noticeable in the gathering, were a large contingent of uniformed policemen all wearing a symbolic black arm band. Some officers from the district's police post including Corporal Donovan, were also present, however there were no sign of Sergeant Webber.

Corporal Donovan and Sergeant Webber share a good working and social relationship. Sergeant Webber was his training Sergeant at the police training school and have since taken a great liking to him. Corporal Donovan was seen as special by his colleagues as he was the only police in the force to penetrate that social wall of Sergeant Webber.

Freddy and Mally were already present. Freddy took the microphone from the chanter and tries to solicit everyone's attention. When this was achieved, he began the proceedings with a prayer.

Praying for the bereaved family, protection and safety for the attendants and the district at large, he concluded by asking God to render swift justice for the victim's family.

Denise, Sheila and their families have just arrived and are embraced by some of the people standing at the entrance to the yard. As they get closer inside, Denise was further embraced by John's mother and other member of the family.

The festivity heightened, the drink flowed endlessly, the band was in full swing and the jumping and prancing went on erratically. The revelers sweated profusely in the crowded and temperate atmosphere.

Suddenly there was a gush of extremely frigid air followed by a strong aromatic floral scent and a power outage. These extraordinary events lasted a couple of seconds and had everyone dumbfounded momentarily. People in these deep rural districts usually have a deep belief in the preternatural and the chanter immediately demonstrates this by demanding the crowd to sprinkle more rum on the ground to satisfy the thirst of the spirits.

Normality returns and the ceremony rolls on.

The fearful and frightful look on Denise's face caught the attention of Freddy who was standing about a meter away from her. He came over to her and asks, "Are you ok?" "I'm ok" she replied. With Freddy's training, he sensed that she was troubled and insisted that they move to somewhere quiet to converse.

Denise readily acceded and so they both take a walk up the road. If there was anyone, Denise felt comfortable talking to, it was Freddy. She related, in chronological order the series of events to Freddy, starting with the shivering of the Kasha tree at the James's house when John spilled his drink onto it and again when both she and Freddy were in the company of Mr and Mrs James, the dreams and now the recent sensory phenomena.

Freddy was quick to dismiss any thoughts of paranormalism from her head and offered a theological solution instead in the form of a lengthy prayer.

Feeling a bit more self assured, Denise thanked Freddy as they both walked back to the Wake.

Back at the police post, Sergeant Webber, in protest of the complaint against him, has decided not to attend the Wake. All the other team members are working at the Wake to keep the order and a watch on proceedings. Sergeant Webber sat at his desk in front of a wide opened door ready as usual to entertain all complainants. With his transistor radio and service two way radios on his desk, he kept himself entertained while being alert and ready to respond to his colleagues on the road.

Suddenly the music stopped, the light inside the office starts flickering, a sweet floral scent permeates the air, and a cold chill replaces the warm interior.

Not a man who is easily flustered or frightened Sergeant Webber remained calm and waited out the phenomenon which lasted a couple of minutes. As if nothing had just happened, Sergeant Webber sat there around as calm as possible. Five minutes later, the security lights around the perimeter of the post all went out and the metal gate closed with a mighty slam.

Now this got the attention of the Sergeant who removed his nine millimetre from the holster took it off safety and was in full preparation mode. He picked up his radio to call for backup but found the radio unresponsive.

The office lights starts to flicker rapidly, the temperature in the office dropped sharply.

The Sergeant was, maybe for the first time in his life fright filled. While the light flickered like the inside of a disco room, the Sergeant noticed an image resembling that of a tree at the front door. He began firing in that direction but only manage to get off two rounds. His fingers were numb and could not respond to the dictate of his brain. He was speechless and motionless as he was now held in a spiritual grip.

He was attacked viciously and pierced all over his body. All this happened within a couple of minutes. The lights then came back on and the two way radio and the transistor radios regained functionality.

No one heard the shots from the Sergeant's gun because the entire district was at the noisy Wake.
Several hours later the Wake wound down and people began departing to their various destinations.

Corporal Richards, one of the on duty policeman at the Wake, and who is assigned to the police post, tried to make radio contact with Sergeant Webber. Several attempts from the corporal proved futile. He tried the Sergeant's mobile phone, however it rang unanswered. The Corporal relayed his actions and obvious suspicion with the other colleagues who, without delay, set out for the post. Upon approaching the main gate to the post, everything seemed normal, with no evidence of foul play. However as they reached the office entrance door, they were greeted by a mutilated body, matching the physical profile of their senior officer and boss, lying face down covered in blood and blood stains everywhere.
His gun was still clutched in his hand. The desk seemed to be undisturbed, with only a few spots of blood evident. A few green leaves were also seen on the ground in the centre of the doorway.

One of the policemen vomited on spot, others were shaken and in tears. They were too shock to execute the force's standard procedure. After regaining composure, one of the police proceeded to alert the officer on duty at the Mandeville police station. At this time none of the resident knew about the incident. Within minutes after issuing the report to the police station, the scene was swarmed with police and later, with reporters and some curious members of the district. Within an hour of the incident, the scene at the police post was chaotic and the police in charge of the scene struggled to keep the onlookers at bay.
The processing of the crime scene continued in earnest, and as day broke, the magnitude of the reality set in.

Reporters from all over the island representing all the media were on hand scavenging as much data as they could. Specialist teams of forensic experts, investigators and government officials including the minister of national security were present. In an on the spot press conference, the minister of national security described the incident as a sad day in Jamaica at this time and that no resources would be spared in bringing the killer(s) to justice.

Inside the office, the investigators processed the scene, they turned over the body and observed that the Sergeant's mouth and eyes were wide open as if frozen in a pane and preserved in time. Doctor Reynold was already there to pronounce the victim dead and to execute the usual formalities before the body was removed by the undertakers who were now becoming very acquainted with the district.

"This is the third horrific killing in the space of a month which has grappled this usually quiet district, how do you plan to put an end to these horrors and reassure the residents that they are once again safe?" Asked one reporter. "At this time, the government has employed some of the country's finest crime scene operatives and is committed to soliciting assistance from overseas if the need arises.

We are hoping to make a breakthrough in all these cases as soon as possible so we can restore normality to the district" the minister responded. "Mr Minister, in the meantime, how can you reassure the residents of their safety?" asked another reporter.

"We will immediately increase our resources in the area, including more patrols. There are other policing strategies which the commissioner will deliberate on later." the minister responded. "Mr Commissioner, why are the first two cases still unresolved?" ask a reporter

"Well, those cases have proven to be a mammoth challenge for us, however, let me hasten to say that they are not insurmountable and we will reach a resolution in short order" said the commissioner.

"Sir, I was reliably informed that in all the cases including this one.

You were not able to recover any weapons, neither were there any unexplained footprints or fingerprints, or even a single eyewitness. Are we dealing with supernatural events here sir? A reporter asked. "Let's not get above ourselves here, as I said earlier, the cases provide new challenges for us, but this will only serve to strengthen our resolve and I want to stress the need for calm at this time and implore you all to assist the police with any and every information possible. No more questions" said the commissioner as he walked away from the reporters.

The MP then addressed the people. "Beloved citizens of this quiet district, your lives have been disrupted by a series of tragic events within the past month. As the Member of Parliament for this division, I want to express, on behalf of my government, our deepest sympathy to the families who have suffered from these injustices.
We mourn with you as we share your grief. Being the Member of Parliament for this area, I am absolutely sure that these ghastly acts are the works of outsiders. This district has always evinced a high spirit of brotherhood. This district has never needed the services of the police to mediate in social conflicts or petty crimes. There has never been a murder committed in this district in the past. The people of this district epitomize the concept of social cohesion.

We want to urge you once again to be vigilant, continue to be your brother's keeper and give your fullest cooperation to the police who will be working in your district for weeks and maybe months to come until we arrest this untenable situation. We are asking you not to be crippled with fear by these series of events, but go about your normal daily task but with a greater sense of security. Thank you."

Mass Ballack's renegade team was growing in numbers and was desperate to preserve their district status as one of the most peaceful district in the country. They held their own meetings and although not oblivious to the cautions of the police, the group was hell bent on dispensing justice their way. Several nights have passed and the group had yet to observe any threatening nocturnal activities. The set up night time camps in the bushes at several points inside the district. Each camp had at least four "soldiers" all armed with machetes and wooden clubs.

The objectives were well defined, the goal was common and the commitment was strong. Each evening they would meet at Mr Alexander's shop just before nightfall to have a drink of rum and to get a fresh supply of cardboard boxes. The cardboard would serve as flooring as they stay low between the bushes with watchful eyes. It's Friday, and one full hour before John's funeral service commences. The Red Berry SDA church is a fairly large building, with a seating capacity of over two hundred Though fairly well supported, the only time the seating capacity is reached and exceeded, is the hosting of a funeral, school graduation ceremony, special district meetings, political meetings or other special events. As it drew closer to the commencement of service, the church was expectedly filled to capacity. As much people were on the outside as there were inside. The church had put in place contingency measures for such situations. Deacon Malito James ordered the church overseer/and grounds man along with other volunteers to erect tents outside in the church yard and furnished them with chairs from the store room.

Like a well drilled staff, the operation was swift and efficient. Most people were by now seated and awaiting the start of the service. Noticeable in the congregation, were media reporters who were at the crime scene recently and policemen elegantly dressed in their funeral fatigue which is black pant with a single broad white stripe running laterally down each leg, a white tunic.

Some more decorated than others with badges of honour. The constabulary sewn on badge, epaulettes on the tunic, a white peaked cap with the constabulary force's emblem firmly positioned at the front, a well polished black congress boot, a black dress belt with gold plated buckle bearing a full colour badge, and white gloves to round it off.

Pastor Grashan (Freddy) and two other clergymen from Kingston were the officiating pastors and were already seated inside the pulpit. The coffin was still open to the congregation's viewing of the body. Pastor Grashan then moved to the microphone to get the ceremony under way. All the formalities proceeded and the funeral was in full gear. A few members in the congregation were tearful as they all sang hymn after hymn with an interlude of tributes from family and friends.

Denise read the eulogy with a less than smooth delivery as she paused several times to re-gather strength. It was a tussle to the end and was anyone's bet if Denise could complete the eulogy or emotion would render her speechless. In the end, Denise managed to be the victor. With tears flowing freely down her eyes, she was assisted to her seat at the front among John's family. Denise tears seemed to have precipitated the bursting of the Dam as most of the congregation was now flooding the church with tears.

This segment of the ceremony was over and the congregation was now on the march for the interment which is just a few metres away from the church. At the graveside they sang as they lowered the coffin into the ground. Within an hour John was laid to rest. The attendants were served refreshments and a hot meal, in keeping with tradition and custom.

People gathered in groups reflecting and discussing the day's event, they were cognizant that at least one more funeral was in the pipeline in a couple of weeks. People departed for home in different directions while the faithful few headed for Alexander's for their usual Friday night booze.

Some of the elders from the district went by the last crime scene to view activities there only to find the police post and the immediate surrounding confines decked in yellow and black tape with the writing "POLICE DO NOT CROSS." It was now seven o'clock and the district was like a ghost town which is uncharacteristic of Red Berry on a Friday night. The only place with some amount of activity is the main shop, which was by now, well populated with the renegade team led by Mass Ballack. They were gulping down their final drink of spirit before heading for their various camps.

Just before the team departed, a police patrol car drove up to the shop and the officers urged the residents to be extremely careful on the streets and politely asked them to go to their respective places of abode. Like well trained soldiers, the renegade team separated themselves into the pre-arranged groupings and headed for their camps without the cops having the least idea what was going on. It was approaching midnight, and the only sounds that could be heard was that of beetles and every half an hour or so, the patrol car.

Denise was too tired to join the group on watch, and thus would not be able to do so again until Friday night of the coming week. Her friend, Shirley spent the night over at her house to offer her moral and emotional support. They both played a game of card poker in Denise's room over two cups of premier Jamaican Blue Mountain coffee and Water Crackers. Sheila had taught Denise how to play Poker a few years ago, however their skill level is just about equal at this time. After couple of hours playing, they both retired to bed.

Sometime after falling asleep, Denise was awakened by a cold gush of wind which rushed through the half opened top window; she arose from the bed and closed the window. The room was unbearably cold so she moved towards the wardrobe for a blanket.

As she pulled open the door of the wardrobe, she saw tree-like object bearing limbs similar to a human. She tried screaming but there was no sound, she was frozen in a spot as if she was glued onto thin air; this paranormal phenomenon lasted only a few seconds. When she was extricated from this grip, she made a loud scream. Both parent rushed to her room while deep sleeper Sheila tossed a few times and went back in deep sleep mode.

Her mom hugged her while her dad carried out a frantic search of the house.

Armed with his machete, he checked the windows and doors for signs of entry. His search was thorough and no area of the house escaped being searched. Several minutes had passed and Denise was still shaken. Her mom went to the kitchen and prepared some hot chocolate beverage, while Denise sat on a chair in the corner of the room with her dad consoling her.

Mom returned with three cups of the hot beverage on a platter. She fetched another chair and placed it within touching distance of the other two. After a couple of sips, the warm beverage seemed to have defrosted the frozen pane in which Denise was held.

She related her experience to both parents without the fear of being psychoanalyzed. She boldly related all the dreams and the personal experiences with the Kasha trees. She was now in full vocal flight as her parents listened without interrupting.

"All this is brought on by the death of John" her mother stated, "you see" her mother continued, "when a person loses a loved one, they manifest different psycho-emotional responses, they have visions they can't explain.

They sometimes claim to see things, similar to what you're experiencing right now." She explained. "No mother" Denise shouted angrily, "I am not imagining things what I saw was real, I am not crazy" she assured her mother.

"I did not mean to offend you" her mother quickly inserted while embracing her closer.

"What's happening here?" asked Sheila who was now more than half awake and sitting on the bed. "Is there something wrong?" Sheila insisted. "Everything is fine, Denise just had a bad nightmare" her dad said quickly. This immediately drew a look of assent from Denise, who in return gave him a wink of the eye. She readily interpreted this response and action of her dad as one of concealment from Sheila.

Denise was offered the choice of sleeping with her parents, but promptly refused. She felt much better than several minutes before. She was now alone with Sheila, sitting up on the bed and chatting. Sheila tried every trick in the book to eke out information from Denise, but without success.

It was now, a couple of hours before day break and sleep had now eluded both Sheila and Denise.

Meanwhile, in the other room, Denise's father Godfrey had a bad feeling about what his daughter had recently recounted. Godfrey, unlike his wife Gloria, will give credence to the supernatural world.

Trying to build a case for justifying Denise's perceptions, Godfrey, like a well learned detective, started to put the pieces together. The revelation of Denise's two experiences with the Kasha tree beside Eric's Tomb seemed to have sparked his recollection of that eventful day when Eric and Erica were both mowed down by the car.

He recalled arriving on the scene shortly after the incident. Erica's body was about a meter from the car while Eric's body was another several meters away pinned up between a dense shrub of Kasha trees. He also remembered assisting the police in trying to retrieve Eric's body, and the difficulties they encountered. Eric's right hand clutched onto one of the Kasha trees firmly and provided the team a major challenge to relinquish his grasp.

His body had multiple punctures from the Kasha thorns.

Godfrey was also integral to the construction of the Tombs and the grills at the James's home.

Revealing this for the first time to anyone, he told his wife he had noticed then, that within the space of two weeks after the James's children's burial, a Kasha tree appeared beside Eric's tomb. "I assumed that no one else seemed to have realized it, because no one has ever mentioned it" Godfrey asserts. "Please lay these theories to rest and promise never to mention them to Denise, you will only scare her" Gloria pleaded. 'Of course dear,' Godfrey respond sarcastically. "I am serious Godfrey" Gloria insisted. "Ok, Ok" Godfrey reassures her.

Daylight descended on the district and police investigators were back on the scene at the police post combing for clues. One could not help but notice a team of "white" men wearing white overalls with the letters FBI boldly written in black at the back of each overall. There were six of them working as a team with some of the investigators who were working the scene the day before.
The presence of the white men drew the attention of people from the district who were out in their numbers. They spoke with high British accents, much to the fascination of the locales in the district, who were still restricted from venturing too close to the scene. The local police on patrol in the district told some of the enquiring residents that the white men were forensic experts from England, and took the opportunity to remind them not to cross the yellow and black tapes.
The British operatives would from time to time take a brief respite to refresh themselves with water and snacks by the Alexander's shop. While there, they would interact with the residents and even treat them to a few drinks.
For the third straight night, Mass Ballack and his renegade team yielded no result and some members were becoming despondent and started contemplating an abandonment of the team. The team had to rethink the strategies and come again. A meeting was proposed for the weekend to examine and discuss same. The members agreed, and then departed their separate ways.

Mally and his wife Angella were running a bit late for Sabbath service which was about to begin, as they were delayed watching the British men along with some of the local police combing the scene in front of his house where Bigga mutilated body was found. It seemed as if the British men were visiting all of the crime scenes. Denise and Sheila along with Gloria and Godfrey were also running late as they walked down the road just behind Mr and Mrs James.

While passing the James's resident , Godfrey and Denise looked across at the Tombs into the yard and noticed that the Kasha tree was not there. He was not alarmed by this, as he thought to himself that Mr James must have chopped it down. Denise, who may have had similar thoughts like her dad, kept it to herself.

Mass Ken was tired after being on the watch out the entire night and could not attend church service that day. He spent the entire morning sleeping. His sons Kenny and Kenneth usually do a great job with the chickens. Kenny ordered Kenneth to go into the town to purchase feed for the chickens. Kenneth took the family truck and left for the town of Mandeville.

There was a large order to be delivered that very same day at a wholesale grocery store in the town, so all the preparations were put in place by Kenny.

A team of workers came over to assist in the killing and plucking (de-feathering) of the birds. Kenny organised some of the men to prepare the fire for the water to start boiling. He along with two other men went into the woodland in search for dry wood to fuel the fire. While in the bush, they split up in different directions. Kenny armed with a machete chopped his way through the thick undergrowth to access a pile of dried woods.

As he finally made his way to the pile of woods, he heard a swashing sound behind him like leaves beating on the ground. The swashing sounds immediately stopped as he looked around frightfully. To his astonishment, he realized that he was surrounded by a ring of Kasha trees.

He was perplexed by the experience and started chopping frantically for an exit. The ring began closing in; Kenny was motionless and speechless while still being conscious. He was attacked by the trees in turn each inflicting puncture wounds with deadly effect.

Kenny's lifeless body lay there in a pool of blood. Afterwards, the Kasha trees moved back to their original location with only small branches and leaves of the Kasha trees at the scene.

The other two men who went with Kenny were on their way back out of the wood calling for their boss.

They set off back to the house thinking that Kenny must have gone ahead of them.

When they returned to the house, they asked the other workers if they saw Kenny.

All the persons there replied in the negative. Some of the other workers were beginning to get impatient as they needed Kenny's directives in order to pursue other tasks. This absence by Kenny is seen as strange. Kenny is a great organizer who normally leads his "troop" efficiently. He would never abandon a job in an incomplete state. Sensing that something maybe wrong, a team of persons formed themselves into a four man team and set off into the woods in search of Kenny. Led by the two workers who initially went with Kenny to the woods, they all set off in the direction where Kenny was seen heading.

Suddenly, one of the workers points to an object several meters away which resembles a human lying face down on the grassy mat of the woods.
They approached the object slowly with great apprehension and caution. As they drew nearer, the worst becomes apparent.
Without the need to have any scientific identification done, everyone on the scene could tell that it was Kenny's body lying there.
The scene was typical to what they have experienced, and now gotten accustomed to over the past month. Now saturated with fear, they huddle close together while looking around into the woods assessing its' safety status.
Not wanting to separate themselves from the group, two of the men suggested that they should all go back to the house to alert the rest of the workers.
They all agreed and moved with fear and caution back to the house. Before reaching the house one of the men bellowed out that Kenny is dead. The workers rushed towards the wood and onto the scene. Some of the ladies began crying openly, while others were muted by shock.
A few of the workers returned to the house to inform Mass Ken. When they got there Mass Ken was still asleep while his wife was attending the church service.

One of the workers who is a close friend of the family awoke Mass Ken and temporarily crippled him with the horrific news. Mass Ken hobbled out of the yard, still clad in his pajama and bedside slippers. A shock filled Mass Ken had to be assisted as he moved into the woodland. By this time, the news had spread rapidly across the district and within minutes the place was crowded with residents, police, and the British investigators, who were still working a crime scene several hundred meters away. Not before long, the media were in town as if anticipating the event. Doctor Harry Reynold arrived as he usually does and pronounced the victim dead.

The hearse arrived one full hour later and removed the body for the morgue, but not before the scene was thoroughly and meticulously processed. There were enough police in the area to form a human chain link around the district and so they did as they imposed an unofficial curfew. They conducted a thorough search of all the houses, the residents and the bushes in the area in a hope to recover the murder weapon or any evidence which could assist them in cracking the present and past cases.

News of the latest killing has now drawn the attention of the political directorate of the country; the Prime Minister, along with her minister of national security, the Member of Parliament for the division and the commissioner of police.

Their first order of business was a visit to the family house where they met and consoled the Kennedys.

Now swarmed by news hungry media personnel, the commissioner was asked to respond to the mystery killings and the snail past in which the investigations were proceeding. "Our investigating teams have never experienced such perplexities in what appeared to be straightforward case.

The lack of crucial evidence has further set us back in our pursuit for a quick closure to the cases." he stated. "We have employed the services of forensic experts from England to assist us in our investigations.

We have also increase the security resources in the district.

It is our intention to reopen the police post in short order and we are committed to working assiduously in order to dispense justice to the families of the victims and to make the district a safer place" he assured the gathering.

The prime minister did not escape the media as she was asked to comment on the crisis facing the district. "The government wishes to, first; publicly extend our deepest sympathy to the relatives and friends of the victims.

We will continue to support the police in their efforts to combat crime in the district and in the entire length and breadth of Jamaica" she uttered. "I have already demanded a comprehensive progress report from the commissioner of police and will brief the nation on the state of security in the country including the Red Berry horrors.

In the meantime, I want to urge you all not to quilt under the weight of these horrors but to act in unity to fight this recent scourge. Thanks, that's all for now" she said, as she walked away. The residents, who by now felt exasperated beyond endurance, were now beginning to experience an emotional transformation.

Their tears were suspended as if they had developed an immunity to cry. The once quiet and peaceful residents were now beginning to exhibit boisterous behaviour. Even the strongest adherents to the Christian faith, had began to molt that Christian armour. The modality of the protest was rapidly changing to a violent fracas as there were verbal clashes between some of Mass Ballack's renegade team-mates and the police, who were painfully restricted in their usual use of force, by the presence of the official government and police hierarchy.

The raging residents were tranquilized into calmness upon the delayed arrival of their dear pastor Freddy Grashan who chose to address the gathering.

"My people" he said "don't allow the devil to possess you into violence, we must continue to demonstrate the spirit of brotherhood and peace, we must continue to pray and ask God for strength and guidance at this time of great sorrow.

Most importantly we should work with the police, as only a united effort can bring about a speedy resolution." Those were Freddy's words as he made his way to see Mass Ken and the rest of the Kennedy family. On his way Freddy was met and greeted by the departing prime minister and her team who applauded him and urged him to continue his great work in the district.
Inside the Kennedy's home the mood was sombre and the investigators were still interviewing Mass Ken and his family.

Freddy dialogued with a few of the residents who were in the yard, trying to get a report on the tragic event which occur there earlier. The residents were void of emotion as they related the incident to Freddy, who was now joined by Mally and Max Archer who was back into the island after a one week trip abroad.

After the police ended their interview with the Kennedy's, Freddy along with Mally and Max proceeded inside the house to offer support to the family which was now extended by the arrival of Jeremiah Kennedy, the brother of Ken. They expressed their sincere condolences to the family followed by an impromptu prayer meeting led by Freddy. Other senior members of the district join the meeting as they sang and prayed. This spiritual healing had a positive effect on the Kennedy's, who for the first time since their son's death, managed to exhibit any form of physical strength as they moved to and from the kitchen and the bathroom unaided.

They provided refreshment for the small gathering.
Already pledges of cash and kinds were being made to facilitate the expected Dead Yard activities. The wealthy Max Archer had committed a whopping one hundred thousand dollars to assist with the funeral expenses and another fifty thousand dollars for drinks. The expression of gratitude temporarily masked the sorrowful facial wan of the Kennedys. Other members of the district chipped in with their pledges as a symbol of support which is typical of the district.

14

Jeremiah lives in Waterhouse, a politically fractious and often time's violent district. He lives with his two daughters Jean and Joan, ages twenty one and twenty three respectively; students at the University of the West Indies; both pursuing Management degrees. They are very close to their father having lost their mother several years ago. Jeremiah owns and operates a grocery shop in his district and is well respected by the residents there. He organizes an annual football/soccer jamboree in the district where members of the adjoining communities participate.

This was done in an effort to promote peace and foster a greater social relationship among the political divided groups. Jeremiah is a successful business and family man and immediately demonstrates that at his brother's home.

He had contacted the Wholesale in the town, which had placed the order for the chicken, and apologised for the non-delivery while explaining the reason. He had committed to deliver the order the following Monday. With the help of his nephew Kenneth, he began to put things in place in order to ensure a seamless operation and an on time delivery.

It was now Sunday morning.

The sun was just beginning to peep out from the heavens; the atmosphere bore a total contrast to evening before. The sweet smell of fresh flower blooms permeated the air. A gentle breeze blowing by the willow created a whispering melody which harmonised with the chirping birds which resulted in a perfect duet. The lush green vegetation, interspersed with a plethora of brightly coloured flowers, and dampened by the overnight dew created the perfect back drop for nature lovers.

The scenery changed rapidly as the morning got older. The beautiful melody was now replaced by the sounds of human, animals and the police service patrol car which was doing its daily round in the district.

Mass Ballack was seen leading his cattle into the woods, while Mally and other residents were seeking wood to use as fuel for cooking.

The sound of machetes was heard hitting against trees and small shrubs as farmers were actively working their fields.

The activities in the district increased as the investigators continued on with their tasks working in tandem with the forensic experts.

Sunday is generally a wash day for most residents in the district and Denise was at it while receiving help from Sheila. There is no laundry room inside the house, so laundry was done at the back of the house.

Denise and Sheila used three large plastic basins, one with soapy water in which washing is done, another which has a fixed position under the pipe, with plain water for rinsing and another for placing the rinsed clothes after removing most of the water by wringing. In other areas of the district where there is one standpipe serving several residents, they would all congregate close to it and wash in turn while feasting on some juicy gossips and topical issues.

Others sing too as they wash, to lighten the heavy wash load. Generally speaking, wash day is usually fun filled in these rural districts.

Gloria didn't participate as usual in the laundry as she was busy trying to complete a suit she had started earlier that week.

Godfrey was inside his workshop sitting and pondering over the recent spate of events and was bent on putting a preternatural twist on it as he postulated.

Denise and Sheila were almost finished. Denise's schedule was a packed one. She had to prepare a lesson plan for her class and assist in the preparation of the dinner. Due to her interrupted sleep pattern last night, she was already struggling to keep awake. Sheila was coping a little better and advised her to take a short nap while she started the dinner.

Noticing the silence inside the "workshop" where Godfrey was, Denise went inside to check. She saw Godfrey staring out in space and seemed to be in a daze. "What's the matter dad?" she asked "Just thinking" he replied. "What about?" Denise insisted. "Well, the killings, your dreams, and both of our experiences" he uttered.

"I am sure the police will bring about a closure to these killings soon, while at the same time apprehend the perpetrator(s)" said Denise.

"This is much bigger than the police to handle" a concerned Godfrey warned. "What do you mean by that, dad?" a panicked Denise asked while drawing herself closer to her father.

"This is a long story and you're looking tired and may need some rest" Godfrey responded, Denise insisted that her dad reveal his knowledge to her, but being the stubborn person he was, Godfrey insisted that he will disclose everything to her in due course. Denise departed the room disappointed and headed for her room where she was quickly engulfed by fatigue and thrust into deep slumber. Later that evening, the Boland's family, like many of the other residents in the area, were preparing to attend the Dead Yard at the Kennedy's home.

Before departing the home with his wife, Godfrey ran a meticulous security detail on the house, ensuring that all the points of entry were secured. Denise could not attend because she had to complete her lesson plan for school the next day. Sheila opted to stay and keep her company.

For the first time, Denise seemed to be struggling with her lesson. Her concentration span was regularly interrupted by her recent mysterious experiences. This was obviously noticeable that it prompted Sheila to enquire about her friend status. "I am ok, maybe it's fatigue, I am sure it's nothing to worry about" Denise assured Sheila.

Sheila, being quite aware that pressing for more suitable answers would be an exercise in futility. As Denise struggled on, Sheila watched helplessly but still with some optimism that Denise will complete her task in short order so she can engage her in a card game.

15

At the Kennedys, many of the residents were out in great support of the bereaved family. The domino and card games were already in progress under the large tent into the yard, while some members were on the inside conversing with the Kennedys. The James and the Greshan family had just arrived and immediately organised a prayer meeting.

The games were suspended while the prayer meeting ensued. The singing of gospel songs and the prayers lasted for nearly an hour after which the games resumed. Cups of hot chicken foot soup were served, which was shortly followed by beers and white over-proof rum; tap water was the popular chaser for the white rum in these neck of the woods.

For the younger drinkers of white rum, coconut water and coke were the preferred choices. In these rural districts, the consumption of rum is like a daily ritual and span over a wide age range. It is strongly believed that the white rum offers protection from evil spirits, however, as mentioned earlier, to receive the protection one must release a few drops on the ground to appease the spirit.

Then, and only then, will the protection be granted. Drinking white rum to the point of intoxication gives the feeling of courage and subsides any fear of danger. Another valuable attribute of rum, is that it creates a social adhesion which unite the district, and keeps friends together.

It rids the mind of problems and creates a stress free state. This state of nirvana, however, only lasts for a short time as it is removed by soberness. As if reading their minds, Max Archer arrived with a case of 1 litre white over proof rum and a similar case of red rum, which he took straight inside the house; much to the disappointment of the crowd.

He came back outside, went into his car and took out four bottles of white rum which he left on the outside to be consumed by the appreciative crowd.

During the peak of the activities, Godfrey summoned a meeting with Freddy and Mally. They sat around a table at one corner of the tent with their glasses of rum and water. "Gentlemen, it has been a sad period in the history of our district," Godfrey said. "We have seen several gruesome deaths, all of which are shrouded in mystery." He continued. A bit unsure how and when to introduce his preternatural postulations, he wittingly enquired about their opinion on the subject. "I believe that the killer is an outsider (from another district) who is familiar with the district" Mally said with some amount of confidence. "Well I do share the same sentiments" Freddy added, but not with the same conviction and confidence as Mally. Both responses had made it more difficult for Godfrey, who sought some assistance from the reliable rum and water cocktail. "Well, I have a different theory to these killings" he said as he took a couple of gulps of the confidence booster. He started by asking some questions. "How is it that there are no foot or finger prints on the victims?

How is it that there seemed to be no evidence of the victims struggling before their demise? And how is it that there are no blood trails in any of these cases?" Godfrey asks as he sipped from his glass with more regularity.

He had the full attention of both gentlemen who were now muted and having optical fixation with each other. It was a perfect time to launch his attack. Godfrey started to tell both men about Denise dreams and her recent experiences, he reminded both men about the tragic day when Eric and Erica died and the difficulty he had relinquishing Eric's grasp on the Kasha tree.

With Freddy and Mally still muted, Godfrey continued without even pausing for another sip as he wanted to maintain the psychological advantage he now has over the men. Godfrey made mention of the Kasha tree leaves at the scene of two of the victims and the "disappearance" of the Kasha tree beside Eric's Tomb and its reappearance the day after. All three men requested a refill of the precious cocktail in a bid to regather themselves.

Both of the clergymen were in no mood to observe their drinking limit as they all craved assistance from the glass of rum and water.

"The investigator revealed that the killer uses the Kasha to camouflage himself" Freddy remind Godfrey. "Why would someone use Kasha to camouflage himself? Godfrey asked. "He would inflict damage on himself with that choice of camouflage, I believe the investigators are scratching for answers and as a result have delved into the ridiculous. I
t is practically impossible for someone to cover himself in Kasha, attack and over power his victims, and lay low in bushes without seriously damaging himself" Godfrey said. "Are you saying that the Kasha trees are responsible for the killings?" Mally asked, boldly.
"Yes, that's exactly what I am saying" Godfrey replied confidently.

"Well, it's getting late and I think it's' time I head home" Said Freddy who was getting very uncomfortable. "Me too" Mally said, adapting and employing Freddy's exit strategy. Both gentlemen gathered their wives and bid farewell to the Kennedys and the other residents. They were joined in their departure by other residents and they walked together in a group away from the Dead Yard.
Not a word of the disturbing conversations was uttered as they walked home to their respective homes. Two police men armed with their weapons, walked with the group to their destinations. The moon was shining brightly and the air was still. The sounds of the beetles were prominent while the fireflies exhibited their radiance as they kept company with the group.
On reaching the James's home, both Freddy and Mally looked towards the Tombs where they saw the Kasha in place standing in place as still as the night's air. As Mally and his wife went indoor, the rest of the group continued on their merry ways.

Back at the Dead Yard, activities were winding down and most of the residents had already left. Kenneth and his uncle, Jeremiah began organizing the clean up with the aid of a hand full of people who were still around, including two policemen who were standing guard in front of the yard. The other members including Godfrey and his wife left in a group with the two policemen as escort.

Denise and Sheila were still awake and unaware of the time as they enjoyed several games of poker. A heavy rapping on the door elicited a scream from Denise that instantly served as a catalyst for a louder scream from Sheila. "Denise, it's Gloria and your dad" a reassuring voice said.

Denise opened the door and let her parents in. Gloria tried to calm her daughter's fear by assuring her that the police were combing the area tirelessly. They even accompanied us from the Dead Yard" Gloria told her.

As Gloria tried to allay her daughter's fear, Godfrey stared on in a complete daze as he found himself in a potential family conflict.

Wanting to impose his theory on Denise but was quite understanding of the consequential overtones, he thought that going along with his wife's understanding of the situation would be the better way to go. After a prolonged conversation of assurance on the matter, they all retired to bed.

16

That night while the four policemen sat inside their service vehicle
on full alert, they received an emergency call on their CB radio.
They were informed by the command post that some men, heavily
armed were heading in their direction. They were instructed to
intercept with caution.

The police team then set out to execute their duty just as they were
instructed. They used their car as a barrier, positioning it across the
main vehicular entrance to the district and stood guard as they
awaited the villains. The sound of several cars was heard
approaching the district. Three cars; two of which were police
service vehicle with their flashing blue light and blaring sirens, were
now in full view and approaching the barrier at a threatening speed.

The policemen behind the barrier took evasive action and
positioned themselves in safe but strategic positions. The villains,
realizing that they are now cornered, turned their car off the road
and into the bushes that lined both sides of the road. They then
alighted their vehicle and ran in random directions inside the
district with the chasing pack of policemen and a number of rounds
in their pursuit. The now frightened and already rudely awakened
residents were trying to get a piece of the action by peeping
through their windows.

Some of the resident could see the flashing blue light on the police
vehicle directly while others could only see the light through the
bushes. Many of the residents had a sense of security knowing that
the police were involved. "I hope that the police capture the killer"
Freddy whispered to his wife who was also on the lookout.

Gunshots traded between the twelve man strong policemen and
the four villains.

One of the gunmen, now out of ammo and had no bearing of his
direction laid low in the bushes hoping not to be captured or killed
by the lawmen.

As he laid there in terror he heard the rattling of bushes coming in his direction. With no effective weapon, he chose to make himself as small and inconspicuous as fright would allow him. He felt a very, unbearable frigid chill, followed by an entire numbing of the body. With his eyes wide open, he saw a treelike object towering over ten feet in height and appeared to have human limbs (hands and feet) over him.

Helpless and unable to cry for help he conceded his inevitable fate. The treelike object descended upon him and pierced him hundreds of time with its overextended thorns. He succumbed immediately. The treelike object returned to its original position and back to its natural state. The shootings continued, with most of the shots coming from the police weapons.

A suddenly muted Maria tapped Freddy nervously on his right shoulder and indicated, to him by gesture only, that a man was in their yard. They both watched the man whose profile was very visible under the moon lit sky. He moved and stood beside a guango tree, however he was still in the view of the Grashans.

They watched him as he looked up towards the heavens in search of divine intervention. Freddy and Maria continued to look on without a blink, as they saw two towering treelike images approximately twenty feet tall and having hands and feet pounced upon the man, now obscured by the treelike images Freddy and his wife could not see clearly what was taking place.

There were no sounds except for the switching of the trees which were very erratic in their movement. The trees then moved from its prey and into the direction from whence they came. The man was still there lying motionless on the ground. The Grashans stared at each other motionless and speechless in a state of shock.

After several minutes elapsed, Freddy broke out of the spell and tried to relinquish his wife from her state. Unable to understand or even to explain what they had just experienced, they both quietly got out of bed and headed towards the bathroom in response to their fear induced bowel movements.

The couple washed their faces and went back to the window to ensure that the event they had just experienced was real. The man was still lying beside the guango tree motionless.

Meanwhile, realizing that they were the only ones shooting, the policemen observed a self imposed cease fire as they continued to search the bushes armed with flash lights and guns. More police from other police divisions arrived and joined in the search and to expand the dragnet.

The other two villains were still moving aimlessly inside the bushes. They were together and determined to escape. Like trained soldiers, the two men moved away from the advancing police men whose positions were betrayed by their nervous chattering, the trotting boots and their flash lights.

As the villains moved away from the advancing policemen then encountered dense vegetation ahead of them and watched helplessly with swollen heads as the vegetation enveloped them. There was no escape. With a few rounds left in their guns, they fired wildly at the enclosing trees.

The policemen who were some distance away started firing away wildly in the direction where the firing was seemingly from. The execution of the two remaining villains was swift and frightful. The flora status of the woods returned to normal after the incident. The pursuing policemen were joined by another team of officers as the search intensified.

The search lasted for several hours before success was achieved. The last two villains were the first to be found. They were both covered all over in blood, as the police gave each other the high fives. They radioed the police high command to report on their success.

The search continued for the other two whose bodies lay in different sections of the district. It was now daylight and the district flooded with policemen. The other two bodies were founds a couple of hours later in similar conditions to the other two.

The residents were asked to stay indoor by the police as they conducted their investigations.

Some of the residents could observe the removal of the bodies by the policemen. The members were kept informed of the situation by way of mobile contacts with each other. The common speculation going around the district was that the serial killers that have been stalking the district were now dead. The news spread joy across the district.

Denise and her mother held hands and said a prayer of gratitude to the Most High. Like most of the residents, Denise was in celebratory mode and was awaiting the chance to leave her home and mingle with the rest of the district.

Godfrey and his recent convert Freddy were not in such mood as they had other theories. Unable to function due to the shock inflicted by her latest experience, Freddy had to prepare breakfast. Maria just sat on the sofa silently as she descended into the abyss of the thought world. Freddy held her and proceeded to go through a marathon prayer with her. The prayer had worked and Maria was back to the surface with all her cognitive functions still intact.

During breakfast, Freddy proceeded to tell Maria about the conversation he had with Godfrey the night before. Maria had never questioned her husband's judgment in the past. However sensing that he was inclining towards Godfrey's paranormal theories, she insisted that they should both leave the matter in the hands of the Lord.

Freddy, showing great respect for his wife, and not wanting to increase the perplexities of her mind, which was now in a quandary, desisted from discussing the incident any further.

17

The hearse arrived with the undertakers, Doctor Harry Reynold was already on the scene along with all the forensic teams. Media personnel were on the streets working along with the police covering the stories of the event as they unfolded
The bodies were later removed and taken to the morgue.

Later in the day as things unfolded, the residents were out in the street in their numbers as the police had earlier lifted the restriction on the residents that had kept them indoor. The Red Berry Primary and Infant school was ordered closed for the day, while some of the shops in the area remained closed.
The Blue shop was later opened and immediately transformed into a conference centre. Many of the residents had gathered there discussing the earlier events while craving for some information from the better informed residents. Most of the policemen and the forensic teams along with the media were already out of the district.
The four policemen who were assigned to watch and protect the district and who were involved in the earlier engagement with the villains were replaced by four other policemen as their shift came to an end. The residents at the Blue shop were joined by the policemen on patrol.
They received a warm and congratulatory welcome from the residents. Corporal Donovan who was a member of the patrol team informed the residents of the recent events that took place in their district. A he spoke; the residents realized that the men who were killed may not have been the person(s) who had been plaguing the district with terror. This new revelation served to re dampen the residents' spirit taking them from a joyful high to a despondent state. The killing of the four men had however, not only given the residents a brief sense of pseudo security but also hope.
Hope because the police demonstrated strong resolve and a commitment to rid the district of that new born terror.

The Kennedys was one of the families which were greatly affected by the occurrences of last night's events. They were celebrating on hearing the earlier report from some resident that the killer was shot and killed by the police.

There was supposed to be an address to the nation by the Prime Minister and Minister of National Security on Sunday of that week. With the Red Berry horrors expected to headline and dominate the discussion. This had placed the police high command under extreme pressure to produce a report in such short time. Adding to their complexities was the fact that the post mortem on the recently deceased bodies has revealed that none of the four villains were shot, the modalities of the deaths were identical to the previous deaths in the district. The British forensic team had conceded defeat.

They admitted that they have never experienced such a case in their many years on the job. One of the Englishmen referred to the case as phenomenal and unnatural. The local forensic officers and investigators were also at a loss.

This admission by the British team had firmly placed some members of the police high command under the threat of expulsion. Now under extreme pressure, the Superintendent of police along with some of his high ranked officers had decided to go back into the district to speak with some of the residents. The Dead Yard would provide the perfect setting as most of the residents would be present there.

The residents were already gathering at the Dead Yard in their numbers. The scent of the chicken foot soup was distinctive and pervasive as it seemed to have stained the air with its aroma. Kenneth had bought party ice and some disposable plates and cups to facilitate the expected bumper crowd. The high ranked police party had just arrived much to the surprise of some of the members.

They met with the Kennedy family, where they exchanged cordialities. They seized the moment to procure permission to have a meeting with residents.

The permission was promptly granted. Word of the proposed meeting spread like wild fire throughout the district prompting residents to cancel all other plans and make themselves available at the Dead Yard.

With the Dead Yard now overflowing with people the Superintendent of police for the Manchester division asked for their attention. "We are here tonight to seek your help," he said as if on begging knees. "Our investigations so far have not led us closer to solving any of the cases, we are still not able to determine the number of persons involved in the recent murders, and furthermore, there are no murder weapons recovered and no DNA signatures.

What makes it a bit more complicated is the fact that the recent killings in your district of the four men several hours ago, bears similar resemblance to all the killings which preceded it. None of the four men that were killed earlier was shot. They were all found dead with multiple punctures all over their bodies. We have earlier theorized that the killer used the Kasha bushes to camouflage himself, however this is almost practically impossible to achieve. I have deployed policemen in your district on a twenty four hours basis in an effort to curb the incidents of crime but that has proven to be futile.

I need to know if any one of you witnessed any of the crimes, or see anything which may be of assistance to our investigations" he asked.

Everyone was dead silent as the Superintendent moved his head slowly from right to left making cursory glances on the gathering as he did so. His plea for help was sincere, and his humility compelling. Freddy looked across at Godfrey who then looked across at Mally. "Please" the police officer begged, I need your cooperation on this one. "You can speak with me directly or any of my officers during the course of the night." He added.

Soup was being served along with the district's favourite cocktail; beer and pop soda were also served.

Freddy and Mally came over to where Godfrey was sitting. Freddy spared no time in resurrecting the discussions they had abruptly put to rest last night.

Freddy told the two gentlemen what he experienced last night. A smile replaced the concerned look on Godfrey's face as he finally got a supporter in his corner. Mally was at a loss for words as he listened to both gentlemen. The problem both Freddy and Godfrey had, was to disseminate this theory without risking being ridiculed by some of the residents. Freddy, being the leader of the district felt compelled to share his experience plus Godfrey's postulations. Both Freddy and Godfrey tried to convince Mally that they should go as a group and try to seek audience with the Superintendent. They took a couple swigs of rum and water to gather some confidence and restore some courage. "Sir, can we move to a quiet area to talk" Freddy asked the Superintendent.
The Superintendent had previously met Freddy and knew of his reputation and a response in the affirmative was inevitable.
They entertained into the luxury of the Kennedy's living room. Godfrey preluded the discussion by telling the officers of his postulations and at the same time trying to convince them citing facts in each of the cases. "Gentlemen you may have had a little too much to consume" a senior officer uttered, while having a cheeky smile on his face. "As Godfrey proceeded unfettered, the noticeable grin on the officer's face slowly disappeared and replaced by a serious facial wan.

"When Godfrey told my about his theories, I too thought he was crazy even with some logical deduction cited" Freddy said bravely. "I confirmed his theory when I witnessed the killing of one of the four men last night" Freddy continued. The officers were fully attentive and as serious as judges. "My wife and I looked through the bedroom window and witnessed two trees having manlike features and approximately twenty feet tall move up to the victim, who was unable to react, and with a few minutes of rapid agitations the treelike object walked away" Freddy recalled.
This revelation by Freddy had the effect of causing the eye of the officers to bulge while at the same time prying their mouths open.

No one who knew Freddy was going to question his integrity as his reputation preceded him. Both sides were quiet for a while as they took several sips from their glass. The theory makes sense and seems to be the only explanation which is flawless. "The problem is how can I present this explanation to the minister of national security, I would be fired forthwith" the Superintendent said. "We will have to find a way to prove this theory. "We need to find an Exorcist "the Superintendent remarked.

"I know how to get a hold of one" Freddy exclaimed much to the delight of the Superintendent. "How quickly can you get him" asked the Superintendent. "By tomorrow" Freddy replied. "That's great, let us all meet here tomorrow at noon and devise a plan then" said the Superintendent. "Gentlemen it is within the district's best interest that we keep our discussions and plans confidential" the Superintendent said.

Freddy along with Mally and Godfrey all shook hands with the officer, then returned to their previous seating positions. The officers were still sitting and chatting among themselves. All the officers were not on one accord with this as some began to envisage the difficulty in trying to convey this to the commissioner, and worst the minister of national security who was a highly devoted Christian.

"Even though Godfrey's postulation sounded compelling, it was the pastor's claims that pushed me over the belief barrier," the Superintendent said as he stared deeply into the eyes of one of the main detractors to the recent theory. "We have to provide solid proof in order to convince the minister and the commissioner" one of the officers uttered. "That is why we have to devise the best possible plan when we meet with the exorcist.

The Superintendent along with his team departed the Dead Yard bidding farewell to everyone they did so.

Corporal Donovan came over to where Freddy, Mally and Godfrey were sitting and requested permission to join their company. Having been granted his request Corporal Donovan said"

I could not help but overhearing parts of the discussion you were having with the officers."

Looking Freddy deep into his eyes as he continued, "I saw a strange twitching of the Kasha tree in Mally's yard, which caused my head to swell resulting in a period of brief disorientation, Denise also witnessed the same phenomenon.

I could not even respond in the affirmative when Denise pressed me for an answer. I was in denial since, not wanting to even think about it. Something broke free inside of me when I heard you speaking about your experience and so I felt compelled to come over and share this with you" "Great" the Pastor asserted "it is not healthy to bottle up things inside of you" he warned. "We are having a special meeting right here tomorrow can you make yourself available?" Freddy asked. "We need as many testimonies as possible" "Ok" the Corporal gladly accepts.
Please remember not to mention this to anyone" Freddy said in a firm tone, determined to keep it a top secret, "you got my word on this" the Corporal assured him. It was getting late and the residents had decided to call it a night. They departed in two groups and were escorted by the police patrol team, as was now becoming customary.
This was the second consecutive night that Denise's sleep was not interrupted by horrific visions or any supernatural manifestations. As a matter of fact, her sleep last night was the most comfortable one she had ever had in years. She had already done her morning chores and was now getting ready for work.
Godfrey was kept awake most of the night by anxiety which was brought on by his perceived expectations of today's events. He was not up and about as usual and this drew the attention of his wife.

"Are you ok love?" she asked, "Not really" he admitted "what's wrong" Gloria asked curiously. Godfrey enlightened his wife on all the recent revelations and admissions and secret meetings.

Gloria, who would normally rubbish these claims, was flabbergasted by Freddy's account. "Oh my God, what are we gonna do?" Gloria nervously asked. "We will be having a meeting later with the Superintendent and an exorcist then I will inform you more. But in the mean time please keep this information confidential" Godfrey implored.

Back at the Grashans home, Freddy discussed the meeting he had with the police officers last night with Maria and told her of the proposed meeting they had planned for later. Maria who would never accept or even entertain paranormalism was converted by her own experience. She supported Freddy's participation wholeheartedly.

Freddy had to travel to a town called Hayes in the neighbouring parish of Clarendon to personally meet with his long time friend and colleague in the ministry Daniel Jackson aka Priest Jacko.

18

Priest Jacko has a towering structure well over six feet tall and weighs close to two hundred and sixty pounds. He sports a bald head which is permanently covered with his famous red tam. He grows a long beard which apart from his eyelash is his only facial hair. He speaks with a heavy bass voice but has the ability to switch to tenor during his chanting moments. The Priest is a well renowned exorcist, who is called upon to solve spiritual cases when other clergymen have failed. His methods are unconventional but his results are positive.

Many people see him as an Obeah man who practiced witchcraft. It was only recently that Priest Jacko resuscitated a teen who was hit down by a motor vehicle and was pronounced dead. It is rumoured that the Priest came onto the accident scene minutes after the accident. A medical doctor on his way to work stopped to render assistance but was only able to pronounce the pulse deprived body deceased.

With the small crowd on hand surrounding the victim and the police keeping them at bay, the Priest walked up to the police seeking permission to pray over the victim. His wish was granted. He walked up to the body, kneeled and chanted life back into the body. Some people claimed to have seen a light entering the body of the boy while the Priest chanted.

The Priest left immediately after reviving the teen, answering no questions as he rapidly disappeared from the scene. He owned and operated a church in the district called the Healing Temple which is mostly attended by people seeking an alternative to conventional medicine rather than those seeking spiritual fulfillment. Priest Jacko attracted two sets of people, the poor and needy who adored him and the "well offs" that despised him.

The Priest is however cool and not easily flustered by negative comments. When it comes to his job he serves everyone equally. He was at home when his good friend Freddy arrived.

From the gate, Freddy could smell the readily identifiable frankincense and garlic as he knocked. "Come in my dear brother" a deep and familiar voice invited.

As Freddy walked further up in the driveway the smell of lime and other spices permeated the air.

Candles were lit all around and a seven strong army of friendly black cats greeted him. "My beloved brother" a fearless Freddy said while embracing the Priest with a firm hug. They both sat and Freddy spared no time in briefing the Priest on the recent incidents and at the same time inviting him to attend a meeting later in the day inside the district. Trusting Freddy as he did, the Priest unhesitatingly answered, yes. Shortly afterwards they set out on their journey back into the district.

On their way back there were no further discussions on the events in the district, but instead they used the opportunity to take a dive back into history. They also had a lot to catch up on as they had not seen each other in a mighty long time. The last time they met was when the Priest wife, who lost her life to cancer, died. That was some four years aback.

They lost contact somehow but never lost the great friendship they had. Freddy took the Priest to his home to see his wife who was also a great friend of his. The inescapably strong essence worn by the Priest caused Maria to start a bout of coughing. The Priest who is also adept at bush medicine told her to pick three leaves from the King of the Forest tree, place them into a cup and poured boiling water onto it. Allow it a few minutes then drink unsweetened. He claimed that this would rid her of her coughs and cold. She acted on his advice promptly.

It was now rapidly approaching the meeting time and Freddy had to leave home along with the Priest. When they arrived at the Kennedys home, the police team along with Mally and Godfrey were already there rapping with the Kennedy family.

Standing on the outside was Corporal Donovan who was waiting on Freddy to formally invite him to the meeting. "Gentlemen, I would like to introduce you all to Priest Daniel Jackson a.k.a Priest Jacko and I think it is important that we invite Corporal Jackson to be a part of this meeting as he will give his own testimony."

All was now set for the meeting. Jeremiah served a round of fruit punch and cheese sandwich for the guests then departed closing the door behind him as he does so. I have already briefed the Priest on the matter at hand.

19

"Sir, we are faced with a crisis situation, both in the district and in our office. It is our desire to bring this horror to an end as expeditiously as possible. You have come here highly recommended and so we crave your expert advice" said the Superintendent, as he began the prelude of what was expected to be a very enthralling and bewitching set of events. "Thank you Superintendent" Priest Jacko roared with a deep voice as he acknowledged the compliment.

"Based on what I've heard from the Pastor, there is an unrested spirit roaming the district, I will need more information in order to formulate the correct exorcism procedures" Priest Jacko added. "What kind of information?" the Superintendent enquired. "I need a profile of all the victims in order to determine if there are any similarities among the victims.

The spirits from the dark world are usually on a revenge mission, targeting the living that may have exacted a similar punishment on them. " Priest Jacko related. "According to our investigation reports, the victims were all male, all well physically endowed," the Superintendent said, but he was stopped in his tracks by the Priest. "No, tell me about their non-physical characteristics" he said. "Were they religious? Were they of similar dispositions? Were they good or bad guys?" the Priest asked.

Getting a clearer picture, the Superintendent suddenly recollected a section of the report which cited the victims as having strong personalities, physically abusive and bullying. Upon receiving this knowledge, the Priest immediately totally changed his countenance. A smile followed by a deep chuckle, which lasted for a near full minute by the Priest planted question signs in the heads of the rest of persons in attendance. "What is it" asked the curious Superintendent. "We are finally reaching somewhere" the Priest remarked. "I have successfully dealt with a similar case in the distant past" the Priest said.

The look of despair on the faces of the police officers was replaced with a touch of glee as the hope for success was becoming more apparent.

"I have a good idea of what I am faced with" said Priest Jacko. Someone inside your district died sometime ago and his/her soul underwent metempsychosis" the Priest suggested.

Can anyone recall the death of any resident having any relations with Kasha trees more than two years ago?" Priest Jacko asked. Godfrey raised his hand, "I do sir" he addressed the Priest. Godfrey gave a detailed account of the incident. "That's it" the Priest joyfully exclaimed. "There is the source of your problem" he asserted. "The boy was victim of abuse and lost his mind and was on the verge of losing his soul before he was hit by the car.

He had a very strong will which is often times mistaken for defiance and insubordination. The constant abuse had pushed him closer to seeking solace from the spirit world. I can tell that this child was very quiet. Just before the accident, his spirit may have commanded the weaker spirit of the driver to send the car in his direction," he summarized perfectly.

Tears ran down the face of Mally as he wept uncontrollably. "Forgive me", he begged as he held on to Freddy. As the police officers looked on sadly, both the Pastor and the Priest placed their right hand on Mally's head and shoulder respectively and prayed separate prayers for Mally.

The prayers worked immediate wonders as it soothed Mally back to a composed state. A grief stricken Mally started to recount his relationship with his son which was in perfect coherence with the Priest's assumptions.

"I will need a number of things in order to accomplish this feat" the Priest said. "You name it" the Superintendent declared, breaking his long silence. "I will need the following" said the Priest, "some special spell enhancing portions which can only be sourced at a Pharmakeia in Haiti, the father of the dead boy has to be placed into my spell in order to form a direct link with the spirit, anyone who has encountered the spirit without being harmed by it, another powerful exorcist and of course money to purchase the portions and travel expenses."

Desperate for quick results and seeing what finally looked like light at the end of the tunnel, the Superintendent pledged to fund the trip and other expenses. Mally, in a bid to try and rewrite the wrongs opted to perform any function called upon to perform. Being quite aware that Denise was the last and probably only person to have confronted the spirit, Godfrey was in a quandary. He remained silent as he struggled with his newest concern. He knew that neither Gloria nor Denise would be in compliance with this. "We still need to find a person who recently came in contact with the spirit without being harmed" Everyone looked around except Freddy who was looking directly at Godfrey with extreme intensity.

Sensing that there may be a possible solution lying somewhere between Godfrey and Freddy, the Superintendent asked Freddy if he knew of any such person. "Yes sir" a truthful Freddy replied. "Who is that person?" the Superintendent asked.
It is Godfrey's daughter" he answered. "Well, with all the requirements within reach we shouldn't have much more of a problem" a resolute Superintendent said. "We may have a problem convincing my daughter to partake in any of this; furthermore her mother may not comply." Godfrey said. "We will have to have to pay the family a visit and try to explain the gravity of the situation" the Superintendent said. "We are running out of time, and so we need to act expeditiously. When can we pay the family a visit?" the Superintendent enquired. "Later today when Denise is home from work" Godfrey replied. "Fine, we will be there" said the Superintendent.
The Superintendent reminded Priest Jacko that time is of the essence and that he needed to move with great alacrity. The Superintendent promised to organise the funds first thing in the morning, he also promised to take the Priest to the airport personally.
Now quite relieved, the police officers invited the men, with the exception of Freddy and Mally, for a drink at the Blue shop. Mally didn't want to drop a bombshell on his wife and daughter so he asked Freddy to accompany him home so that they could set the stage for later. Freddy was the perfect choice for this venture as he was well adored by Gloria and Denise.

20

Gloria was sewing when Freddy and her husband arrived. Sheila was over by her house and so the moment was ripe to be seized. Godfrey spared no time in requesting Gloria's attention. Gloria promptly stopped sewing, came over and hugged her Pastor before her beloved husband. "What pleasure do I owe this visit?" she asked the Pastor. "I am here to discuss a sensitive matter with you my dear sister" he said, wasting no time.

Her smile was replaced by a look of concern. Freddy went on to explain the proposed visit. She knew there were more to it than that and urged Freddy to tell her more. "Later at the meeting we will discuss the real "meat of the matter" he said.

Gloria turned to her husband whose lips were zip locked from the time he entered the house. He repeated what Freddy said. They left shortly after to rejoin the rest of the team at the Blue shop.

At the shop a few residents were just sitting around and chatting, The Superintendent reminded his travelling party not to discuss the case. The policemen and the Priest met the Alexander family for the first time. There were an abundance of handshakes and smiles going around with the policemen seizing the moment to reassure the residents of their commitment to bring this series of horrible murders to an end.

Mr. and Mrs. Alexander were lavish in their hospitality. They brought out extra chairs for the guests and served them slices of potato pudding she had made earlier.

They were given special china wares to drink from and not the usual disposable plastic cups that the residents normally used. Mrs Alexander didn't stop there; she presented two bottles of Grgich Hill Cabernet Sauvignon red wine to the guests. "This is on the house" she said wearing a smile as she did so.

A police from the touring party called Mr Alexander aside and cordially advised him to look about the spirit licenses as soon as he possibly could. Mr Alexander promised to do so.

They ordered drinks for everyone while showcasing their domino skills. Both Freddy and Mally joined them later and phased smoothly into the activities.

The scene resembled a typical Saturday night at the shop. The crowd grew and so did the festivity. It was like a district treat. They organised a domino tournament with police against civilians. Six domino tables were brought out from the store room for the six teams. Freddy decided to officiate the proceedings setting the rules as follows: six games will constitute a match, the loser of a match will be eliminated, the finals will be a battle between the last two teams standing, silence throughout the games and any signs or gesture made by any team member, which the judge interpreted as coding/cheating would result in that team being disqualified.

After the first round of games, it was predicted that the finalists were going to be the police team with the Superintendent and the civilian team with Priest Jacko. The Priest seemed to be a cut above everyone else; he read the game beautifully and exhibited great skill. The Superintendent on the other hand, though very good, didn't seem as proficient as the Priest; however, his partner appeared to be better at the game than the partner of the Priest.

As was expected, the final was between the two aforementioned teams.

There was a short break before the finals. Members of both teams went and got some fresh air and stretch their muscles in the process. The finals got under way in grand style, with the support split down the middle. The first game was won easily by Priest Jacko's team.

The supporters cheered at the end of the game. The second game bore a similar result. It looked one sided as the Superintendent's team was taken to school by the Priest, who was almost doing this single handedly.

The supporters for the Priest's team had a field day of cheering as their team won all six games and were crowned champions.

The skill of the Priest was almost mystical.

No one there had ever seen such display of domino mastery. Priest Jacko and his team member were awarded with handshakes from the losing team and from Freddy, and another complimentary drink at the Superintendent's expense.

After a few hours, the time had come and the ten man crew departed to visit the Bolands. The arrival of the crew, in three police service vehicles drew the attention of Sheila who was still by her house.

Two other neighbors who lived in close proximity to the Bolands were quickly outside their house looking on curiously. To avoid a gathering of residents at the Boland's home, a member of the police crew went over and informed the neighbours that it was just a casual visit. The explanation was accepted by the residents, who readily retreated indoors. Godfrey introduced the party to his family.

After the introduction, the Superintendent addressed the family. "As you are well aware, there has been a series of unusual, but very sad events which have swept the district over the past month, and which still remain unexplained" he said while looking directly at Denise who was clutching her mother. "The crimes, we believe, are not normal in their characteristics and as such we have chosen to explore other means of bringing about a solution" he continued. "Priest Jacko, is here to assist us in our endeavour, and he has requested a member of the district who recently came in confrontation with what he believes is an unrested spirit and remained unharmed. I will ask the Priest to give further explanation" he said as he looked to the Priest.

"Spirits operate in two distinct modes, similar to a light switch which is either on or off with no in between. The spirit will harm you if it dislikes you and spare you if it likes you" he explained. Once you have come face to face with the spirit, regardless of its manifestation, and it doesn't harm you, it will never harm you in the future.

You are one of a few persons who can communicate with the spirit, which will be an essential part of the operation" the Priest explained. "In order to make a spiritual connection (a bridge) between the spirit and the exorcists, we would have to put you in a state of enchantment, we also may require Mally as a bait for the spirit" he further explained, but was interrupted by a hand raised by Gloria. "What danger does this pose for my daughter and what is the purpose of the bait?" "No danger at all to her, as a matter of fact if we don't successfully put the spirit to rest, then your daughter will be visited by the spirit on other future occasions, also, the killings in the district will continue.

We believe that this spirit is very strong and so we will need all the assistance to remove and capture the spirit" he confidently explained. "Please, we need your help," Freddy begged. I will be there close to you throughout it all" he assured. On hearing Freddy's plea and getting his assurance she nodded in approval. "When will this take place" she asked. "Day after tomorrow" the Superintendent asserted.

Getting the approval, the Superintendent and his team were further delighted, Godfrey and Freddy were relieved. Denise received a hug of appreciation from the Superintendent. The team discussed the plan meticulously then left the Boland's home. They dropped off Mally first. There they looked intently at the Kasha tree standing quite unassumingly in the proposed site for the exorcism. All three cars shut off suddenly, simultaneously and refused to start after several attempts.

All the occupants came out as the drivers opened the bonnets in an attempt to rectify the problem. A few minutes passed and they were still not successful. The Superintendent asked one of the officers to fetch his CB radio. When he got it and attempt to call for assistance he realised he wasn't getting anything from it. It was as dead as a door post.

The Priest, realizing his was beyond the ordinary, raised both hands above his head and chanted a prayer in a language no one there understood. At the end of his chanting, the cars all started by themselves and the CB radio's functionality was restored. They all, with the exception of the three Captains clustered together in a state of lethargic inertness. "The spirit is on the roam and will more than likely kill tonight," the Priest said to his frightened team-mates. He suggested that Mally could be the next victim and advised him not to sleep in the district until the exorcism was completed. The Priest convinced the couple to visit their family in Mandeville. They packed their bags while the team waited in the cars a bit more assured with the powerful Priest in their presence. "Our task is not going to be an easy one, the power of the spirit is very strong, and I may have to invite a powerful spiritualist from Haiti," the Priest warned. "Can you contact him before you get there to confirm his inclusion" the Superintendent asked.

The Priest searched his phone for the spiritualist number and was successful in locating it. He successfully made contact with the spiritualist and used the opportunity to speak with the exorcist who happened to be where the spiritualist was. The Superintendent promised to make the flight arrangements and the accommodations for the men from Haiti. Luckily, this also meant that the Priest didn't need to make the trip as was planned.

"I will purchase two return tickets for the men, and also remit money to the men to purchase the potions first thing in the morning the Superintendent promised. After dropping off Freddy and Corporal Donovan the officers left the district. They took Mally and his wife into Mandeville and carried home the Priest. "The day has worked out well, despite the brief scare at Mally's home," the Superintendent said with great relief. He reminded the men again of the need for confidentiality. It was a sensitive case.

21

It was time for another night at the Kennedys and the crowd was growing at a moderate rate. The domino games were on in earnest, the menu had changed from chicken soup to mannish water.
Now, Manish water is a soup made from the head and tripe of the ram goat with lots of garden vegetables to provide a tasty flavour.

As usual, rum and water was the dominant cocktail. The crowd was separated in different groups discussing different agenda.
Freddy, Mally and Godfrey were noticeably absent from the crowd, as they were tired, having been out with the team of officers earlier today. The nights' event proceeded without incident.
The residents of the district had retired for the night and were now in deep slumber. The moon was still in its full state and the fireflies were out in their hundreds displaying their optical wares. The sounds of the crickets and other insects seemed to have superimposed into one loud coherent stream. The only other competing sounds were those of the patrolling police car moving around slowly in the district and the intermittent chattering of its occupants.
At the Bolands home, the night's tranquility was suddenly broken by a loud scream coming from Denise's room. Both Godfrey and Gloria rushed inside the room frightfully. Denise was sitting up on the bed in the consoling arm of a trembling Sheila, with her eyes and mouth wide opened as if in a comatose state.
Gloria rushed over and sat beside her on the bed while Godfrey checked around for any signs of forced entry. Both parents, having already experienced a similar occurrence, were a bit less frantic. The prepared hot chocolate for both girls and gave her time to recover before trying to extract a statement out of her. In the meantime, Godfrey told Sheila that it was just another bad dream. "No" Denise shouted, "it was him, I saw him standing over my bed" she uttered boldly.
"See who" a frightened Sheila asked. "Let us discuss this in the morning, I will leave the light in your room on" Godfrey interrupted.

"I want to talk about it now, I am no longer afraid" a seemingly confident Denise said. "He woke me up by tapping his leafy hands on my back several times. I rolled over on my back, opened my eyes and saw his bushy face. He said the words *kalyteros filos* three times then disappeared" she said. "I tried to scream while he was rumbling the words but must have had vocal seizure, it was after he vanished that I was able to scream out." Denise continued. At this time Sheila's fright filled eyes were roaming the room, apparently looking for any thread of evidence that may be responsible in startling her friend. Both parent, satisfied with the state of their daughter's faculties, departed the room.

The look on Sheila's face told Denise that she had a lot of explaining to do. "Denise wasted little time in delivering the narrative, reeling off the events as they happened in chronological order. "So why you?" Sheila asked, referring to the spirit's visitation rights to her." I don't know" Denise replied. "Maybe he is sending me a message" she proposed. "What message?" Sheila asked. "I don't know, but I hope to find out this coming Thursday" she replied. "What is happening this Thursday?" a relentless Sheila asked. "I am sorry but I can't tell you" Denise remarked. "Come on Denise, we are best friends," "Yes and that is why you should respect my position. I made a promise not to reveal anything of the proposed event until it is completed" Denise uttered while 'eye-balling' her without a blink. "Ok", a conceding Sheila said with disappointment written all over her face.
It was a couple of hours before daylight but sleepiness had long gone from the girls, with no intention to return any time soon. "How about a card game of poker?" Sheila asked invitingly. "Why not, there is nothing else to do" Denise replied.
The second visit of the spirit seemed to have induced courage and alter Denise's perception that all spirits are evil and on a mission to harm and destroy the living. This feeling of fearlessness will only serve to strengthen her resolve for the upcoming task later in the week.

Her air of confidence must have transcended to Sheila, as she too was most composed and relaxed, evincing the duality of emotions (joy and sadness) as the results of the games changed.

The morning sun blessed the earth with its radiant glow, and initiating the diurnal activities as it did so. A few dark clouds lingered in the distant sky, giving the reminder that there was a forecast for scattered showers today. This is welcome news for the farming sector within the district as it has not rained in a while. The residents were up and about doing their daily rounds. Sheila was seen accompanying Denise to school; something she hasn't done of late.

A police car with four policemen aboard had just entered the district, carrying with it a trail of dust. They are here to replace the ones currently on duty. This is done with precision timing on a daily basis ever since the police post was closed. The Superintendent was already on the go, fulfilling his commitment. He had already purchased the return tickets for the Haitians and remitted the money to them. The Superintendent had also made bookings for the Haitians at a popular hotel in the town of Mandeville. The Haitians had also given him their solemn commitment to be there on Thursday morning at the appointed time.

With everything now in place for Thursday, the Superintendent paid the Priest a visit to put the final touches in place to ensure that things go as planned. They had planned the event for midnight on Thursday, and were hoping that everything was in place by midday on Thursday. They also wanted to keep it a secret from the other residents; however they envisaged a slight problem. The Dead Yard activities usually finished at about that time.

The fast thinking Superintendent said he needed to have a meeting with Pastor Grashan and the Kennedys.

"I want to ask the Kennedys to have an early termination to their activities on that night" he said, sharing his plan with Priest Jacko.

"If that doesn't work, I may have to ask a specialized police squad to organise a meeting by the Blue shop with the residents for at about eleven o'clock that evening and have it extending beyond midnight" he pronounced while wearing a broad smile.

"The regular police on duty in the district, should not be a problem; I will dispatch them out of the area until after midnight" he said while nodding his head in acknowledgement of his brilliance.

The Superintendent departed the Priest's company and headed for the district to discuss his plans with Freddy.

When he arrived at the district, he met with Freddy who was at the church. He told Freddy about the potential threat to confidentiality and explained to him his plans to remedy the situation. Freddy smiled as he listened, and seemed to be in partial concurrence with the officer."I think we should try and encourage the Dead Yard activities to go on beyond midnight, try to make it a special night so as to get every resident in attendance.

Then place your officers at the gate to prevent anyone from departing early. You may also need to cordon off the area and inform any enquiring residents that a special police operation is in progress" The Pastor said to a suddenly ego deflated Superintendent. "That sounds like a better plan" the Superintendent humbly conceded. The Pastor invited the superintendent to join him in a word of prayer. They held hands and prayed. "Dear God, I come to you as one of your humble servants, begging for your guidance in our proposed endeavour.

Please instruct our every move, so that we may achieve our primary objective. Take us in the palm of your hand and shield us from all evil forces. Please remove danger and harm from our pathways. Please heal the wounded and cure the sick among us. Please replace our sadness with joy, our pains and grief with comfort, our despair with hope and our evil thoughts with good thoughts. I pray for the families of all the victims of the recent wave of horror which have swept our district. Please redress their loss with swift justice. All this I pray through Jesus precious name amen."

The Superintendent shook hands with the Pastor then departs his company, and also the district.

The spiritually enriched Superintendent headed for his office listening to a series of gospel songs from one of the compact discs he carries around in his vehicle.

22

Mass Ballack and his group, still possessing a strong inclination for revenge, vigilante style, had to halt their plans to resume their camping out activities, due to the recent shootout between the policemen and the villains. Thinking that they could have been caught up in that deadly situation, they have decided to rethink their strategy. The majority of the renegade team, with the exception of Mass Ballack, had decided against the camping out.

They instead believed that staying in the safety of their homes while looking out through their windows, for the slightest evidence of human activities was a better alternative. At the sight of a suspicious activity they would devise an alarm system that would alert the team members into action. After several attempts, the right wing arm of the group finally convinced the Mass Ballack led left wing to accede to their safer proposal.

The day was moving at a rapid pace, and it was soon nightfall. This meant time for the Dead Yard. Freddy and the Superintendent along with a few police officers who are a part of the exorcism team all met at the Kennedys.

The police team brought along with them several cases of white rum, beer and pop sodas. Their intention was to have Thursday's activities at the Dead Yard prolonged and the best way of achieving this is to have a constant flow of liquor. The Superintendent also brought along a separate case of white rum which he intends to use a prize for the winner of a domino tournament he planned to announce later when most of the residents are there.

It was the right time for the announcement the Superintendent thought to himself. He first sought and received the approval from the Kennedys.

"Ladies and Gentlemen good night, tomorrow night starting at eleven o'clock, we will be having a domino tournament right here. So get your teams together from now and sharpen up your game, because the winning team will be awarded with a case of whites" said the Superintendent.

This was followed by a series of "oohs" and "aahs" from the crowd, "All participating teams, must register before midday tomorrow to avoid been omitted." The Superintendent warned. "Is there a prize for the minor places?" one resident asked. "No, it's a winner take all competition" the Superintendent replied, much to the dissatisfaction of the crowd. "That's not fair" uttered a protesting resident.

This statement had stimulated the other residents into a peaceful protest, expressing a similar sentiment as they do so. "Ok, I will give the runner up team a case of beer." The Superintendent said, while having his right arm in the air above his head with open palm, exhibiting a gesture of defeat. The new announcement by the Superintendent was met by a huge cheer from the crowd.

A second round of soup is being served, while the cards and domino games went on in earnest. Denise, Sheila and Gloria had just made a belated entry which was immediately noticed by the Superintendent who stood up and extended his arm in their direction inviting a handshake. "Good night ladies, it's a pleasure to see you all," he stated. "Where is your husband?" he asked as he looked at Gloria. "He will be coming shortly" she replied. After the brief moment of cordiality the ladies proceeded to go inside the house to meet with the Kennedys. Inside, they saw Freddy and a few elders from the district having a quiet prayer meeting with the Kennedy family.

They immediately partake as they held hands forming a human chain as they prayed and sang a few selections of gospel songs. This meeting went on for another hour. Denise and Sheila went outside after the meeting to mingle with the rest of the residents. They both went into the company of the Superintendent who sat by himself enjoying a glass of white rum and water. He welcomed them with open arms.

Both Denise and Sheila are occasional drinkers of alcoholic beverage with a single glass limit. Their favourite cocktail is red rum and Coca Cola. They will drink wines of most sorts, and rum cream, along with beers. The Superintendent put out the offer to the ladies giving them the choice of rum, beer and pop soda which they have brought with them. Both girls agreed to have a beer. The Superintendent beckoned to Jeremiah who was standing close by. "Would you be kind enough to serve these two beautiful ladies a beer each?" the over-courteous Superintendent asked. "Sure" responded Jeremiah. The beers came shortly after. The Superintendent received them personally and handed them to the girls. Impressed with his level of courtesy Sheila reciprocated the favour with a prolonged eye to eye contact and a suggestive smile.

The optical fixation was broken by a sharp elbow to the side of Sheila by a seemingly jealous Denise. "Oh, I'm sorry" Sheila apologised, staring at Denise as she does so. "Take a grip of yourself "Denise advised her with a touch of anger in her voice. "That's ok, I was not offended" said the Superintendent wearing a smile as he does so. "Do you work at the same school as Denise?" The Superintendent asked. "No, I am not working presently" Sheila replied as she resumed the eye balling session with the Superintendent.

Sensing a bit of tension building between the ladies, the Superintendent invited Denise into the discussion by asking her about her day at work. "Work was fine, however there was an incident where two boys ganged up and fought another boy causing some minor injuries to his body" "Really. So what action was taken by the teaching staff?" the Superintendent asked. "The two boys were taken to the Principal's office while the victim was treated by the school's nurse" Denise replied. Denise, in an effort to direct the Superintendent's attention to herself, took him on a joy ride back into the history of the school, boring him and Sheila in the process. Sheila in the meanwhile, fully aware of the intent of Denise's tactics allowed her to have her way just for friendship sake.

As Denise related, it was obvious that her audience were getting more and more disinterested.

Realizing that her self-defeating tactics were backfiring, she asks the Superintendent to talk about himself. "Well there is nothing much to talk about" said the Superintendent in a modest tone. "What about your workday?" Denise asked. "I was as routine as routine can get, there were no incidents of crime, no accidents or no domestic violence cases reported to my office today" he replied. Sheila broke Denise's monopoly of the discussion by asking the Superintendent about his family; an area where Denise was heading, but with snail pace.

"Well I am married to a lovely wife who gave me two beautiful children Josh and Jane," he said, while reaching for his wallet to fetch a picture of the family.

Both Denise and Sheila were obviously disappointed, as was subsequently revealed in their facial and vocal expressions. "You've got a nice family" Sheila uttered. "Thank for your kind compliments" said the Superintendent. Denise barely looked at the picture and didn't even comment. The Superintendent could not at this time afford to have fallout with Denise.

Godfrey had just arrived at the Dead Yard, and may have just saved Denise from an embarrassing moment, while at the same time preventing a possible fallout between Denise and the Superintendent.

"Great to see you" the Superintendent said happily as he greeted Godfrey. They shook hands and patted each other on the shoulder. The tactful Superintendent invited Godfrey to join them in conversation.

He sought the services of Jeremiah to get a drink for his most recent table guest and saviour and also took the opportunity to refill his glass.

Both ladies still had a far way to go in completing their beer.

"Where is your mother?" Godfrey asked his daughter. "She is in the living room," Denise replied softly.

Godfrey paid slight regard to the nature of her response and proceeded to converse with the Superintendent about a new crime prevention act which was recently tabled in parliament. The Superintendent expressed his views on the act eloquently while trying to involve both ladies into the discussion.

The discussion was fervently ensued as opposing views were traded between both sides which were split down the gender line. Both ladies opposed the act and gave solid points to support their position. Their male counterpart also defended their position with equally solid points. It was also noticeable that Denise's tone tended to border on the uncivil line when directing her response at the Superintendent.

It was obvious Denise was venting for other reasons, but a smiling and well composed Superintendent, allowed his maturity and his professionalism to guide him. With the anticipation of a very long day to come, the Superintendent and the rest of the expected participants for the exorcism event decided to call it a night. The Superintendent and the rest of his police team had offered to accompany the Bolands home.

23

After seeing the Bolands safely in their home, the police team left. As they drove past the James's home they all looked across at the Tombs glowing in the moonlight. "Did you feel that?" One of the policemen asked. "Feel what?" several others replied in unison. "Didn't you all feel a sudden drop in temperature?" They departed the community and headed for their respective homes. "No" the other three men answered. "Your mind must be playing tricks on you" one uttered. "Let me call the Superintendent and find out if he or any member of his team felt any changes in temperature as they passed the house.

The police proceeded to call the Superintendent who was travelling in another car behind and posed the question to him. "Yes we all felt it" the Superintendent said, doing a poor job in trying to mask his fearful voice. "Well gentlemen, the Superintendent and all the other occupants in their vehicle felt it" The three officers that didn't feel the drop in temperature were all Captains in the force. They are Mark Rogers, Devon Jones and Colin Matthews.

They all shared a religious commonality, in that they all attended the same Pocomania/Revivalist Church situated in the heart of Mandeville. They are also part of a lodge movement. As police officers, they all have a similar story which has happened at different times in their careers. Captain Rogers, in his early years in the force as a Constable, along with two of his colleagues were pounced upon by three gun men as they sat inside a restaurant having lunch.

His colleagues were shot dead on the spot. Young Constable Rogers challenged the men and fatally shot then. He recalled that during the attack, all the gunmen who pointed their gun in his direction were unable to pull their trigger and seemed to have frozen as he picked them off one by one. This event is solely responsible for his religious transformation. Captain Jones had a quite similar event in about the same period when Captain Rogers had his experience. This however took place at his home, while he was alone at home. A gunman entered his home and pointed a firearm at him demanding money, jewelry and his mobile phone.

The frightened policeman, who was unarmed at the time, told the robber that he had no money or jewelry at home with him.
This angered the robber who squeezed the trigger several times but was unable to fire off any round as the weapon seemed to stick.
The robber retreated from the house and was never seen again.

Captain Matthews had a different experience altogether. He was involved in a motor vehicle accident six years ago while driving his private vehicle. A drunk driver collided with his vehicle head on, into Colin's vehicle. Both vehicles were totaled and both drivers were thought to have perished on the spot. While the police and the medics were preparing the bodies for transfer to the morgue they heard a sound coming from Colin's body bag. When the bag containing the body of Colin Matthews, was opened he was gasping for breath. "It is a miracle", said one of the medics who immediately ordered a change of destination to the hospital instead.
Colin was severely battered and broken up by the collision that the doctors thought that even if he survived, he would be in a vegetative state for the rest of his life. He was in a coma and all the vital signs were not encouraging.

After a couple of weeks, Colin had regained consciousness and was exhibiting great audio-tactic responses. His improvements thereafter were deemed miraculous as CAT scans and X-Ray imaging showed unbelievable results. After two months in hospital, the earlier written off Colin Matthews was as good as new, walking about. Free of physical restrictions, and talking with almost cognitive perfection.
Like Mark and Devon, Colin believed he owed this miracle to the Lord and wanted to express his gratitude by becoming one of his humble servants.

Mally and Angella were becoming homesick and were eager to return to their humble abode. They prayed earnestly for success for the upcoming event which was planned for Thursday. The Priest's insinuations that Mally may have contributed to his children's demise have devastated him since.

He had undergone a series of prayer devotionals since the revelation, with a hope of healing the psychological and emotional scar that it had inflicted on him. Angella had been the supporting rock for her husband. She led him in prayer several times a day.

Both Mally and Angella, although keeping this revelation a secret from the rest of their family, are quite cognisant that a total healing cannot be achieved without a total confession to his family, close friends and his entire church congregation. Angella had already convinced her husband to make that public confession this coming Saturday at church. "Use this as an opportunity to educate other families about the negative impacts, physical abuse can have on their children. "Angella said. "by doing this, you would not only be contributing to the Church's family enhancement education programme, but also begin the process of self healing" she further advised.

Back at the Bolands, Denise and Sheila argued quietly and amicably about earlier events at the Kennedys. "I caught you flirting with the Superintendent," Denise accused Sheila "Yes, but just a little bit" Sheila replied with a smile. "You didn't tell me you had feelings for him?" Sheila asked. "Oh no, not at all" Denise denied. "Oh, come on, even the blind could see that" Sheila insisted. "Your actions were loud and clear" Sheila continued. "What actions? Denise asked, "Your sudden change in disposition, your elbow to my side and your unusual aggressive tone when addressing him." Sheila replied. "I am not aware of any change in my disposition or tone, and I only gave you the elbow because I thought you were making him uncomfortable. Denise explained. "Whatever" Sheila responded with a touch of sarcasm.

She knew that Denise was always a tough nut to crack, and trying to pry information out of her will be an effort in futility. They both decided to terminate the argument and retire themselves to bed. Later that night, Denise was awakened by the same tall, tree-like object which she has now become familiar with.

She sat up on the bed vocally and tactically inhibited as she looked face to face with the image, which bent its limb with incredible flexibility, similar to a latex balloon filled with air.

This has now brought their eyes in the same dimensional plane. The moon light peeping through the window panes in the top half of the windows, only allowed for vague visibility. Denise was overcome with a great sense of calm, courage and inner peace as she looked into the ruby red glowing eyes of the image.

It was like bush coming together to take on the shape of a human. There were no visible ears, nose or mouth. It was hollow on the inside and possessed extraordinary long thorns on its outer body.

The only words which it uttered were *"**kalyteros filos"*** which appeared to be coming from deep within its hollow interior. The words were a bit clearer this time compared with the previous encounter. It vanished into thin air after repeating the words three times.

The sensory phenomenon which had Denise in a gridlock had gone, however leaving behind a calm and peaceful aftermath. Denise got up from the bed and stood by the window with the hope of getting another glimpse of the treelike object. She later went back to bed where she slept peacefully until daybreak. The pleasant effects of her experience had carried over into the following day and were noticed by all her close associates, including her family.

She executed her morning chores with a cheerful attitude and appeared to have a greater pep in her step. This paradigm change had evoked a jaw dropping and eye popping effect on the family and especially Sheila who have never seen her like that before. Denise kept her source of joy and inner peace to herself, as her parents and Sheila pondered over her new lease on life.

26

For the Superintendent and the rest of the team, who would be a part of the exorcism, this was the day of reckoning. The usually calm and composed Superintendent was as nervous as they come. This was probably brought on by heightened anxiety and expectations. He contacted the Haitians, who were already at the Port-au-Prince airport preparing to board the flight to Kingston via mobile phone. He contacted Priest Jacko, who had made the necessary preparations for the grand event. The Superintendent also contacted Freddy to consolidate the plans with Godfrey, Denise and Mally and to ensure that everything was going seamlessly.

 He met with the police officers under his command, who were part of the exorcism team and issued his final instructions for the . planned event. Not wanting to leave anything to chance, the Superintendent drove his private car into the Red Berry District to meet with Freddy to have a face to face discussion on the status of the preparation.

Like a well drilled regimentation the Superintendent and the Pastor went through all the plans repeatedly.

Several hours later the Superintendent received a call from the Haitians informing him that they were now at the airport in Kingston. Without hesitation, the Superintendent went to pick them up. At the airport, the Superintendent identified them by the description they gave him earlier.

They warmly greeted each other and exchanged pleasantries as they drove from the airport. When they reached at the hotel, all the transactions were seamless due to the Superintendent meticulous preparations. The three gentlemen met in one of the rooms to discuss the exorcism and to satisfy themselves that everything is in place. It was now midday and twelve hours away from the grand event.

With everything in place, the Superintendent told the Haitians to get some rest as he departed the hotel for his office.

Back in the district, the buzz words were domino tournament. The Blue shop was the scene of bustling activity as several groups of residents were seen discussing teamwork and strategies as it related to the game of domino.

Some teams were seen practicing the fine arts of the game. In these parts of the world, the grand prize of a case of white rum was enough enticement to compel the retired out of retirement, and to get the disinterested, interested.

People like Mass Barry who was once the king of the district, where the game is concerned. He won several trophies in major and minor tournaments all over the island. He stopped playing competitive domino many years ago due to declining health problems. On hearing about the tournament and its lucrative grand prize he was forced to find his friend and many times partner Frank Golding (a.k.a. Mass Frank). These two were fearsome partners in their days.

Going up against them was seen as a foregone conclusion of defeat by many residents. Knowledge of their resurrection and possible participation had evoked fear in some of the competitors while some others believe they had a chance at the beating the once formidable pair.

Both Mass Frank and Mass Barry were at the shop sitting around a domino table trying to recapture their past glory. Their table attracted a few fans who discussed their prowess in the earlier years.

There were other formidable exponents of domino inside the district, but none as colourful as Mass Frank and Mass Barry. The drinking of white rum which was their second nature did not seem to impair them in any way or form as it related to decision making in a domino game, however the reverse was true.

Freddy spend a large portion of the day praying with his wife Maria. This was the first time in Freddy's long pastoral life that he was partaking in an exorcism.

He had read about the subject many times in the past and had seen it in the movies but was still not sure what to expect as most of the cases were dissimilar.

Maria, though strongly spiritual, still had some doubt where her husband's participation was concerned. She too had seen movies of exorcisms and can vividly recall an instance where the Exorcist is killed by the demon. Freddy tried to explain to Maria that his role will not place him in direct contact with the demon, but he will be a member of the séance team.

The Dead Yard was already bursting at its seam with the ever swelling crowd. Additional domino tables and chairs were brought in to supplement the few that belonged to the Kennedys. All was set for what is expected to be an exciting and competitive tournament. The buzz was deafening, as many different groups discussed aloud, varying issues. The superintendent had just arrived with the Priest, the Haitians and the James'. Freddy and Maria were not far behind.

With everyone there and everything seemingly in order, the Superintendent raised his right hand and requested silence. This request was immediately granted. "Good night, the tournament will commence in a few minutes. I trust that by now all the participating teams are registered for the tournament, if not, please step forward and do so now," the Superintendent said. "I have brought along ten of my trusted colleagues to act as judges for the event. I will now introduce you to Corporal Bent who is in charge of the other judges and will manage the entire event." he continued as he called Corporal Bent to step forward and address the crowd.

"Good night residents, I want to take the time to brief you on the rules and the resulting consequence if they are not adhered to" the Corporal said. He proceeded to read out the rules and the consequences. "The structure of the competition will be similar to other tournaments where the losing teams will be knocked out and the winning teams proceed to the next stage until two teams are left. Each match will consist of six games. If there is a deadlock an extra game will be played as a tiebreaker. There will be a ten minutes respite between each match" the Corporal pointed out.

The Corporal went further to explain the roles and functions of the judges and the kind of actions by the players that would prompt a particular action from the judges.

"Is every clear on the rules and the structure? The corporal asked. The non-response was the affirmation that they understood.

He asked for full silence from the audience during the games and explained the importance of their compliance to a fair outcome.

"Now let the games begin" the Corporal announced.

The special team headed by the Superintendent was grouped together as they discussed the proposed event and listened to the experts perspectives on the order of proceedings. The Superintendent made the introduction of the Haitians to the rest of the group. Both Haitian were of similar height and physique, Pierre Soma was the fairer in complexion of the two Jean Vallier had a very dark complexion and wore untrained facial hairs.

Unlike Pierre, Jean was difficult to look at. He had an overgrown beard, moustache and eyelash and not to mention the hair protruding from his nose and ears. His tone was however soft and comforting and was diametrically opposed to his aesthetically challenged appearance.

Pierre had a more commanding voice somewhat similar to that of a military training Sergeant. Pierre, because of his vast experience in exorcism, was chosen to direct the operation. "Based on the briefings I received a couple of days ago, we may be dealing with a very powerful demon that will need to be lured out of its subject. We will need a human link for this assignment" the straight talking Pierre said.

This is the most dangerous part of the process as the aggressive demon exudes its embodiment. "How dangerous?" a concerned Godfrey asked. "Serious damages and even death" the course voice of Pierre replied. "I was told that Denise had been contacted by the spirit at least twice in the past, and was unharmed in both cases" Pierre asserts. "She is unlikely to be harmed by the demon now. Godfrey looked as his daughter with worry and fear written all over his face. "It will be ok dad," a confident and courageous Denise assured him, as she indicated her willingness to take on the task at hand. "We will need someone to act as a bait, someone who the demon is most likely to attack" Pierre said.

The Haitians hadn't had in detail, Mally's abusive past and his possible contribution to his children demise, so Freddy chose to enlighten them. "Perfect" Pierre said. "Mally is the right candidate for the job." Pierre continued.

"Your role is also risky but you will be placed inside a spiritual and physical circle, which the rest of the team excluding Denise will form.

This will offer you greater protection" Pierre assured Mally. "What did you use to flog him during those abusive years? Pierre asked "A whip made from the willow tree" he replied. Are you able to find it? Pierre asks. "Yes it is in my room under the bed" he replied. "Good, we need to get it" Pierre demanded. "Why didn't he harm me before?"

I think you were only saved by your wife. Was your wife the opposite of you where administering discipline to the children were concerned?" Pierre asked Mally. "Yes she was loving and kind to the children who loved her very much" Mally replied with tears running down his eyes."It is the love for her that kept you alive to date, however it was bound to come especially if you physically or verbally abuse your wife. "However, this is not the time for tears, you need to appear to be strong and in an abusive mode as you hold the willow whip in your hand.

You will stand in the middle of the circle holding the whip in your hand. When Denise walks up to you, you will whip her on her buttocks firmly and repeat the exact angry words you uttered in the past while inflicting the blows on him. This re-enactment must appear real. I know it will be difficult for you, but you owe it to your son to put his soul to rest." Pierre said as Mally bowed in acknowledgement.

"We will give you and the rest of the team an edible portion to ingest. This will induce courage which will last up to two hours. Denise declined the officer with a confident smile on her face.
"Are you sure?" Freddy and Godfrey asked simultaneously. "I am sure "a smiling Denise replied. "Denise, you will stand directly in front of the Kasha tree within touching distance but do not touch it" Pierre instructed her.
"What will happen if I touch it?" Denise asked curiously.

"The entire operation will be compromised, you need to create a temptation for him to come out of the tree and into the free world (spiritually speaking)" Pierre explained. "Once you have received the demon, move inside the circle" Pierre repeated, just to underscore the importance of the procedure. "The rest of us will hold hands and form a circle around the bait (Mally) when the spirit attacks him. Jean, Jacko and I will form a similar but smaller circle around Mally" Pierre described. "How will we know when the demon enters the circle?"

The Superintendent asked. It will try and possess Mally then force him to do harm to himself in a revengeful rage. Now this is where all the manpower is needed to restrict Mally's movements" said Pierre. "Mally's strength may increase as much as tenfold, so members of the larger circle should move in to reinforce the resistance of the smaller circle as soon as we beckon for assistance.

Just before we commence the séance, Pastor Freddy Jackson will lead us in prayer, then we will all recite the ninety first Psalm. Priest Jacko will direct the séance chant. Jean and I will take over afterwards. "During the struggle, you must all repeatedly chant the phrase from the spirit ballad which is *ABOUKA GAW ZEN TREP TE CAW*. "What does this mean?" ask the Superintendent.

It is a spiritual command for the demon to leave the body of the living and return to the spirit world" Pierre explained. "The chanting must be done with strong faith and conviction" Pierre warned. "Are there any more questions? Are we all clear on our roles?" Pierre asked.

Everybody seemed ok and set for the arduous task ahead. It was now half past eleven, and nearing time for departure. Freddy offered a word of prayer which consumed another ten minutes then it was time to leave, however there were no clear exit plans. They needed to be as inconspicuous as possible in their departure. The Superintendent instructed them that they should leave in groups of two every two minutes. The feat was not so difficult to achieve, as most of the residents had their minds and eyes fixed on the keen domino tournament.

29

They arrived at the James's home five minutes before midnight. Freddy and the Priest accompanied Mally inside the house, where he removed the willow whip. Back outside, everyone took up their roles precisely, just like well drilled soldiers. Now the moment of truth was at hand. "Repeat after me" Freddy said"whoever goes to the Lord for safety, whoever remains under the protection of the almighty can say to Him you are my defender and protector, you are my God, in you I trust. He will keep you safe from all hidden danger and from all deadly diseases. He will cover you with his wings, you will be safe in His care, and His faithfulness will protect and defend you. You need not fear any dangers at night or sudden attacks during the day" Freddy recites; with the rest of the team giving a harmonious reverberation which followed his every utterance.

At the end of Freddy's recital, Priest Jacko ask the team to repeat precisely the following words: "*The light of God surrounds us. The love of God enfolds us. The power of God protects us. The presence of God watches over us. Wherever we are, God is and all is well. Be our protection against the wickedness and snares of the devil. May God rebuke him, we humbly pray. And do thou, oh Prince of the heavenly host, by God's power, thrust into hell Satan and all evil spirits who wander the world seeking the ruin of souls Amen*".

Jean asked Denise to repeat the following words: "*Oh dweller of the dark world, I invite you to join in our presence. We are here in peace to deliver your soul to a place of eternal rest. Show us signs of your presence*". Denise recited.

Jean ordered her to repeat this until there are signs of the demon with our midst. This first step is the most critical part of the process, without this part the rest of the process will have to be abandoned. After the tenth recital and still no success, Denise went against the script and shouted the words *'kalyteros filos'*.

Denise immediately rose from her feet twelve inches off the ground and spun at about five miles per hour in a clockwise direction, with her hands in full stretch and making a ninety degrees angle with her torso.

This phenomenon lasted for a minute before Denise was released back on her feet. She walked slowly towards the circle with her hands at her side as if she was sleepwalking. Once inside the circle Mally stepped forward and started whipping Denise.

Suddenly the scene became cold and everyone except the three Captains, the Haitians, Denise and the Priest were in a state of stony immobility. The able men formed a circle around Mally who was now fully possessed by the demon. He was frothing at the mouth, his eyes were white with no signs of his eyeballs. The men tried to restrain him while chanting the words   ABOUKA GAW ZEN TREP TE CAW. They could not restrain Mally's demon controlled body and was losing the battle. They were thrown to the grown and Mally was running towards the woods in front of Mally's home.

They regained hold of Mally, who dragged them along in the same direction. Suddenly, Denise shouted the words *'kalyteros filos.'*
This seemed to calm the spirit and the able team regained control and the disabled team members regained their faculties. The total effort of the team managed to have gained the upper hand once again. The chanting of the words ABOUKA GAW ZEN TREP TE CAW was like a scratched record. The chant was with great passion and faith as they helplessly watched Mally gasping for breath as if he was in the grip of death.

Fearing for Mally's life, again Denise ignored the script and stepping from the circle, she placed her right hand on Mally's face and repeated the words: *'kalyteros filos'* followed by the ABOUKA GAW ZEN TREP TE CAW. She did this several times. Suddenly a bright blue light rushed from Mally's mouth. The struggle stopped and normality returned. Mally was breathing normal again, his eyes regained their natural characteristics and seemed to be fully conscious.

30

The job is finished, the demon has been cast out of the Mally and has returned to a restful place in the spirit world. Well done team" Pierre said while staring at Denise strangely. "You saved the day" Pierre told Denise in an uncharacteristically soft tone. "Where did you learn that and what does *'kalyteros filos"* mean?" He asked curiously, while the others gathered around her anxiously awaiting her response. "Well, the last time the treelike image paid me a visit, he looked me into the eyes and said the words *'kalyteros filos',* immediately my fears were replaced by courage and my anxiety by tranquility.

I wanted to speak with it so badly, however he left before my voice returned" Denise replied with confidence and a smiling face. "Why didn't you reveal this to anyone?" Freddy asked. "I told my dad about it" she said. Mally was back to his old self with all smiles as he recounted his tumultuous experience. "I am feeling so much at peace with God and myself. The fear I had yesterday is now gone," he said.

So fearless Mally had become in fact, that he planned to sleep at his home without his wife who was still in Mandeville by his family. "Look," said Godfrey as he pointed to the spot where the Kasha tree was. To everyone's surprise there was no more Kasha tree there. A joyous Freddy gathered everyone to issue a prayer of gratitude to the Lord for the success they had just achieved.

They all headed back to the Dead Yard where activities were still on in earnest. Their re-entry to the Dead Yard was almost unnoticed as the crowd surrounded the domino table The final match of the tournament was in progress and it was between Mass Barry's team and make shift team of Danny Peart, the chef, and Max Archer. The scores were tied at two games apiece.

The games were prolonged by deep concentration before every move. The team of veterans seemed a bit calmer and more confident than their opponent. At the end the veterans prevailed by four games to two.

The superintendent asked for the crowd's attention and got it immediately. "Let's put our hands together for the winner of the tournament" the Superintendent announced. Hand claps and loud cheers followed.

The Superintendent then made the presentations to both teams. Barry gave the supporting crowd four bottles of rum from their prize. With Soup still in abundance, the activities were extended.

The successful exorcism team regrouped and celebrated with soup and liquor. Sheila along with Mrs Boland, Mrs Greshan and other residents joined the team. Both Mrs Boland and Mrs Grashan were relieved on seeing their husbands. They were both eager to learn about the result of the exorcism, but were only told that it went successfully and they will get the details at a more appropriate time. Mrs Boland embraced her daughter and tried to eke out any information she could get on the event. "What are you all talking about " Sheila asked with heightened curiosity. "I will fill you in later" a smiling Denise responded. Everyone was enjoying the moment as if tomorrow would not exist. There was however a look of worry on the face of the Superintendent. "Is everything ok" one of the Captain asked. "Yes, except that I will have a hard time explaining this to my superiors" the Superintendent replied. "Don't worry, you are one of the smartest man I know" the Captain said to the now flattered Superintendent.

The Dead Yard was getting scantier by the minute as the residents departed in groups accompanied by the police. The Superintendent got his colleagues together and instructed one group to take the Haitians back to their hotel, and the Priest to his home. The Superintendent also instructed Captain Mark Rogers to ensure the Haitians had a smooth departure in the morning. He left shortly after with the Captains as his only passengers. This was a deliberate arrangement by the superintendent who was determined to get some explanations on a previous experience.

"Gentlemen, can one of you explain what took place back there at the exorcism? The Superintendent asked. "Could you be more specific sir?" Captain Rogers requested. "None of you three gentlemen were affected by the demon's power, what's going on here?" a curious Superintendent asked. "Well we are at a loss as you are sir" Captain Jones replied with a voice of sincerity. "That day when we were passing the James's house and you all, including our driver, experienced a cold spell except us." Captain Matthews said. "I paid scant regard to it then, but with this recent occurrence, I can only conclude that we might be immune to spiritual evil" the Captain continued. "Why don't you all get a test?" the Superintendent asked. "What kind of test?" captain Matthews asked.

"I don't know, maybe I can ask Priest Jacko." said the Superintendent."I can't be bother with that" replied Captain Matthews. "Why not? Maybe you have got special spiritual talent" the Superintendent suggested. "Well, I will give it some thought sir" he said. "Good and it would be good if the other two men consider same" the Superintendent said in a commanding tone.

"You're right sir. If I discover that I have special powers, this could mean a new career for me which may bring in some well needed revenue." Captain Matthews said. On hearing about the prospect for making additional income, both Captain Rogers and Captain Jones seemed to get renewed interest. If the Priest can test and determine the magnitude of my powers that would be a great start" Captain Rogers asserted.

"We need to make some arrangement to see him" Captain Rogers told his equally ranked colleagues.

"As your manager, I can set up a meeting with the Priest" said the Superintendent with a less than sincere motive. They dropped home the Superintendent and proceed to their respective homes.

It was a beautiful Friday morning, the day after the greatest spiritual event Freddy had ever experienced. He described in fine details, the exorcism event. Just like listening to a well narrated script, Maria was gripped by the suspense filled accounts of the event, as she clung to her husband. Freddy had just came up with an idea to use tomorrow's church service as a platform to announce the exorcism and all the events leading up to it. Maria thought it was a great idea, as it would bring a sense of closure to the recent episodes of terrors inside the community. "I will give the Superintendent a call right now and tell him about my proposal" an excited Freddy said to his wife.

Freddy dialed up the Superintendent. "Good morning sir" Freddy greeted the Superintendent. "I hope the day finds you well and in good spirit" he extended his courtesies. "Thanks you Pastor, and I return the same" the Superintendent replied. "I am proposing to use tomorrow's church service to announce our success in eliminating the demonic forces which have been the source of our horrors in the last month," Freddy revealed.

"I am thinking that you should invite the Commissioner of police and also the Minister of National Security to the service so they can also be audience to this exciting revelation," Freddy continues. "I think I should first brief the Commissioner of the pre-exorcism event and the actual exorcism before making the announcement to the congregation." the Superintendent asserts. "Remember that you only have a few hours to present a report to your Commissioner" the Pastor reminds him.

"My plan is to use the facts from all the forensic reports, along with reports from the investigations to support the pursuit of the exorcism event in the first place and to try and convince him that I have finally put a closure to the case," the Superintendent outlined. "I would like to use you as a reference to substantiate my claims if the need arises." "Sure" the Pastor said. I will set up a meeting with the Commissioner later today, where I will execute this plan, but first I must complete the written report" said the Superintendent.

Later that day, the Superintendent convened a meeting with the Commissioner at his office in Kingston.

During the meeting the Superintendent tried to convince the Commissioner of the supernatural explanations for the killing. "Sir Forensics failed to explain the nature of the killings. It is humanly impossible for a single person to accomplish some of these feats" the Superintendent explained, while the Commissioner nodded in what seems to be a gesture of acceptance to the fact. "Forensics failed to reveal the presence of any human presence on the scene of any of the killings.

All the victim's wounds were inflicted with clinical exactitude, which is almost impossible given the time the assailant had to execute the horrors" the Superintendent insisted. "This is especially true in the case of the three assailants who were killed in a shootout environment with the police.

No human could find the time or the composure to execute this feat with such precision." the Commissioner added, while seemingly concurring with his lower ranked colleague. The Superintendent proceeded to enlighten the Commissioner about the supernatural sightings and experiences of some of the residents in the district.

The well attentive Commissioner was already sold on the Superintendent's theories and in the process, had just inherited the problem of convincing the Minister of National Security. The Superintendent handed over the written report to the Commissioner who reviewed it in his presence. It was a written representation of everything that had just been described. "Let me try and set up an emergency meeting with the Minister for later" the Commissioner said, as he reached for his mobile phone.

"Good day Mr Minister. I have a prepared report on the Red Berry horror you had requested for today, may I come and see you now?" he asked. "Certainly" replied the Minister. "I think you better come along with me" the Commissioner said to the Superintendent.

They both left for the Minister's office which was a few minutes away. At the Minister's office, the Commissioner, handed the report to the Minister without any modification. "Before you read it sir, I think you should listen to what the Superintendent have to say" the Commissioner said to the Minister.

"Go ahead, I'm all ears" the Minister said calmly. The Superintendent again related his account of the incidents in a chronological sequence, almost word for word, as set out in the written report, as if it was a recital.

Unlike the Commissioner, the Minister had many questions which he used to interrupt the fluency of the Superintendent's report. Each question was confidently and expertly answered and prompted nods of approvals from the Minister. "Have you got all this account in the report?" asked the Minister. "Yes" replied the Superintendent and the Commissioner harmoniously. "Well, the evidence put forward in this report is compelling and difficult to defy." the Minister conceded. "I will meet with the Prime Minister tonight at a function she will be hosting at Jamaica House. Well done gentlemen" the Minister stated, as he congratulated the men. On his way driving back to Mandeville, the Superintendent called Freddy and requested that he postpone his announcement until after the Prime Minister's speech.

Without questioning the reason, the Pastor acceded. The Superintendent who was somewhat in a celebratory mood, stopped at one of his famous water holes, Pub Ecstasy, and had a few drinks with some of the regular patrons there.

Back in Red Berry, there was a sudden sense of peace and tranquility. As if the residents had just awoken from a horrible nightmare and all the events of the past month were just a bad dream.

The fears of the residents seemed to have dissipated and the anger and pain disappeared except for the families of the victims. Mr and Mrs James were reunited after a one night separation. Like Maria, Angella demanded a full report of the events of the last few hours. She was a bit more composed than Maria during the hearing of the story.

This was probably due to her more liberal thinking which allowed her to be open to a wider range of views. There were however, tears of sorrow running down her face as her husband recounted the events. "I just can't believe that my poor innocent baby is responsible for these atrocities" she said as the tears flowed. "All the victims were abusers.

He was only trying to protect the abused" Mally said as he consoled his wife. "I have learnt my lesson and I will make this the topic of my sermon tomorrow at church." he said. "Eric had always wanted to protect the poor and vulnerable, he told me several times that he wanted to become a soldier.

He told me that he fought a boy at school who was hitting on his sister" a sobbing Angella said as she unfolded the chapters of his life. "What?" Mally ask. "He begged me not to tell you about it and I promised him I would never betray his trust. I was fearful of the consequences which would befall him" Angella said as she looked Mally straight in the eyes. "I am not mad at you, but with myself. You did what you had to do to protect our son and I am grateful." he assured his wife. "The past cannot be re-written, I felt very bad when the Priest insinuated that my prior actions could have caused the demise of my children.

Freddy and I prayed long and hard for forgiveness, strength and healing and it was at the end of the prayer that I felt renewed. Our prayer was answered and I made a vow then to play my part in eliminating physical and verbal abuse from the psyche of any and everyone I know." Mally said sincerely. "I am committed to continue to work of my son, but in a non-violent way" he continued.

33

Back at the Kennedys, Jeremiah, began preparation to fill the chicken order by the wholesale. He along with Kenneth and Ken got to work earnestly. Kenneth and Ken rounded up support from some of the residents while Jeremiah prepared the slaughter area and the processing counter. He ensured that enough water and firewood were in place. Mrs Kennedy was summoned to start preparing the meal for the volunteer workers who were expected to number about ten. Although ten was the Kennedy's target, this number could quickly rise to twice the amount in the flash on an eye with the availability of a free meal.

The day was travelling rapidly, and was now approaching four o'clock in the evening. This was the time for the routine meeting at the church. The meeting was about preparing for church the following day. Denise, her mom Gloria, Mally, Freddy, Maria and Angella were all expected to attend.

At the meeting, Mally reminded Freddy that a part of his sermon would deal with the subject of abuse. "That's fine" said Freddy, however please don't mention anything about the exorcism" he further added. "Why?" Mally asked, "The Superintendent wants this revelation to be done during the Prime Minister's address to the nation this Sunday. "OK" Mally responded in acknowledgement.

The Superintendent was at his office enjoying some of the most stress free moments he had had in weeks. Having successfully completed and submitted the report without any negative backlash, he had, in the process, transferred the onus onto his superior officers. This was an opportune time to take his long overdue vacation. However being the prudent person he is, he knows that he will have to test the result of his recent endeavour and that could take several months. Although very confident that the cases are now closed, there is still the "what if?" with the accompanying question sign.

Weekends normally represent the grandest times in the community where the hard working folks would take the time out to unwind and relax while putting thoughts of work in virtual suspension. Apart from Thursday night, tonight should have a bumper crowd on hand and the activities should approach fever pitch. The crowd tends to gather a bit earlier, with the exception of the few Blue shop faithful who will trod along later. The features are constant while the attitude of the attendants may vary and this is in direct portion to the depth of the water hole (amount of white rum available).

The sumptuous scent of the chicken foot soup permeates the air in a large section of the small district. The scotch bonnet pepper was very pronounced and these people had a way to prepare it which was beyond compare to what existed anywhere else on the island. One cup of this tasty consumable was never enough and was only out done by the Jamaican white rum. Danny Peart who was there as a part of the volunteer team preparing the chicken for sale, had set up his BBQ grill and was grilling a few chickens to add to tonight's menu. The rest of the team had completed their task and joined the rest of the residents at the front of the yard where most of the activities were.

Freddy would start proceedings with a prayer of blessing, followed by a selection of gospel songs and a few words of encouragement to the bereaved family and to his beloved people of the community. After the precursor, the playing of dominoes and card games would follow the serving and consumption of soups and liquor would fuel these activities, giving reasonable mileage.

Most of the residents had turned out as usual and was making the most of the merriment.

The inseparable pair of Denise and Sheila was in a corner by themselves going bout after bout of poker games. This was their first game for a while and Denise's class was unmatched. Sheila was surprised and dumbfounded by Denise's new found skill set.

There was a sudden roar of cheers as Max Archer entered the gate with a case of white rum, which he handed over to Jeremiah, and instructed him to serve the guests. Today would mark the last weekend that the Dead Yard would be held because the funeral for the deceased would be held the coming Thursday at the Red Berry SDA church. This meant that the Wake would be held on Wednesday of this week.

34

Another day in the life of the community had elapsed, and a new dawn descended. It was early morning, and most of the residents were preparing for church service. The residents were seen making their way to church walking mostly in pairs. The church was almost filled to capacity and service set to begin on time. Seated on chairs behind the pulpit were Maria, Freddy, Mally and two other Deacons from the community.

Freddy rose to his feet and indicated to the rest of the congregation to rise as he began proceedings with a prayer. "Father, thank you for another beautiful day, thank you for bringing us here together safely to praise and worship you. Thank you for health and strength dear God. Please inspire me to disseminate your words correctly and give the congregation the wisdom to understand it. I pray for the sick among us, that you may heal them, I pray for protection from disasters, from evil, from harm and danger. I pray for peace and justice for all. Please grant us success in all our endeavours. All this I pray through Jesus precious name amen."

He then directed the congregation to sit. The church choir sang the selection "*Mine Eyes Have Seen the Glory*".

After the selection Freddy stepped up to the Pulpit once again and started the sermon. The topic of his sermon is "*The Forces of Evil.*" As he went on, he bordered closely on the line which separated the revelation of the events surrounding the exorcism and his present theme. His trademark marathon sermon only lasted a mere sixty minutes this time. He closed his sermon with a prayer.

The congregation was asked to sing the song "*Amazing Grace*" from their hymn books. This was followed by "*To God be the Glory*". After the singing of both hymns, Mally stepped up to the pulpit. Mally's message was a refreshing deviation from the routine service proceedings. Unlike the shouting preaching style of the Pastor, Mally was like good classroom teacher discriminating the content of his message explicitly and in a tone which was amicable and soothing to the audio sensory receptors. He commanded the full attention of the entire congregation.

"I wish to use this opportunity to minister unto you about the values of proper parenting." Mally said in his prelude. He went on about his topic skillfully and in proper text book style without mentioning anything that would breach his agreement with his Pastor.

Though tempted to do so on several occasions, he exercised good control and resisted the urge. At the end of his delivery he received a round of applause which was uncommon. Usually the congregation responds to a good message with "Amen". He must have thought to himself that the moment was ripe for him to make that open confession; but he resisted. The rest of the religious routines followed and the church service for the day came to an end. Mally was the unexpected focal point after the service. Many of the congregants came over and applauded him on a well delivered message. His wife too was very impressed. The post-service attention had further consolidated his belief that he had missed out on a great moment.

Freddy walked over to him and also congratulated him on a great message. A sincere Freddy acknowledged that he may have missed out on a great moment, but the loyalty on a promise must supersede his desire to vent at this time.

Later that day, the streets in the district were quiet as many of the residents were resting while others prepared their evening dinner. As nightfall beset the district, the activities increased, first at the Blue Shop, then later at the Kennedys. The night's activities were typical of the previous nights and they proceeded without any unfavourable incidents.

35

Sunday came; the beginning of a new week. There were no more incidents of terror since the exorcism. Denise had not experienced any more nightmares or demonic visits. The police were still in daily patrol of the district but hadn't had much to report. Many of the residents were now looking forward to the funeral of Kenny and were hoping that this would be the last one for a long time.

Later that same day, the Prime Minister would address the nation. People were tuned in to their radios and television sets to hear the speech. There was a gathering at the Blue Shop by some residents who were there to watch the address live from a television mounted on a wall inside the Pub, while enjoying a drink.

"My beloved people, our nation have been gripped by an escalation of crime in the recent months compared to the same period last year. Many of our people have been the victims of this monster all across the island. Statistics showed that there is a ten percent hike in homicide and larceny, two percent in rape cases and a further 1 percent in other crimes. This is unacceptable, and this government is one hundred percent committed to tackle the problem head on. I have instructed the Minister in charge of National Security to present to me a clear policy document on the topic which I hope to table in the house of parliament in short order."

In the mean time I call on the security force to be fearless and vigilant while at the same time be respectful as they execute their duties within the ambit of the law" the Prime Minister said.

"There have been several gruesome killings in the once quiet and peaceful town of Red Berry district, in the parish of Manchester. These killings were so horrific, that it attracted the international media landscape. I want to hasten to point out that these crimes were not normal everyday crimes.

Our government had sanctioned the hiring of some of the world leading forensic minds in the world. We had also deployed our best detectives in the area to investigate each of the occurrences as they happened.

These detectives collaborated with some of the best investigators across the world via Cyber space.

When I demanded a full briefing, I was informed by my Minister that everyone were clueless. "My beloved people, I am saying that the best minds in the forensic field in the world were perplexed by their finding and had to abort the task prematurely." The Prime Minister paused for impact and took a sip of water before dropping the bombshell.

"What I am about to tell you will evoke different responses from all of you across this country. However, what I am about to tell you, has been proven not only to have provided the only logical explanation to all the killings in the district, but also proven to be the fact." She paused for a second drink of water. "I will ask the Minister to announce the report of his findings" She said as she beckoned to her Minister to take the podium. The Minister was direct and concise as he read the report.

The reactions from the residents in the district were mixed. Those at the Blue Shop, looked at each other, muted by the report. The report had sparked controversy all across the island and soon, the rest of the world. At the end of the report the Minister, as best as he could, tried to convince the residence that their district was now safe and free from the demonic scourge that had plagued it for over a month.

Some of the residents of the Red Berry district were in a militant mood as they demanded an explanation on the revelations from the report and mainly for the secrecy of the operation associated with the exorcism.

Freddy received a call from the Superintendent asking him to organize an emergency meeting at the church later that day where he, along with Mally and Freddy would explain to the residents the new revelations.

The word was quickly spread throughout the district. The Superintendent arrived in the community along with his police escorts, Denise and Godfrey were asked to be there as a part of the official panel which also included Mally, Freddy and the Superintendent.

Things were quickly organized as the eager residents gathered inside the church. The media were unexpectedly on hand.
Freddy began the proceedings with an apology to the residents. He explained quite eloquently the reason for the secrecy. "We had you and your safety at the forefront of our minds", he started. An exorcism can't be carried out in the presence of a large crown or else the spirit would not avail itself, hence we would not be able to cast it out of the living subject and back into the spirit world."

Godfrey then spoke about his suspicions, his speech was followed by Mally's speech, in which he took the opportunity to disclose his confessions of constant abuse of his son. Denise spoke of her paranormal experiences and her involvement in the exorcism. Members of the media were fielding questions, which were successfully handled by the panel.
"Let us use this moment to celebrate our success, we should all go and enjoy a drink and raise our glass to a free and safer community." the Superintendent said. This was met with a loud and prolonged cheer from the appreciative crowd who accepted the compelling explanations wholeheartedly. The Dead Yard was the selected venue. The Superintendent drove by the Blue shop to purchase a few bottles of white rum and other non alcoholic beverages and took them to the Dead Yard. Dominoes and all other activities were delayed as the discussions on the events surrounding the pre-exorcism and the exorcism itself took centre stage.
Most of the younger residents of the district exhibited signs of fear. However, the residents of the district will not be held in bondage by fear, especially the fear of roaming spirits.
The night progressed well and the mood of the residents was positive. It was like getting a new lease on life. The events over the past several weeks had somewhat transformed the community in many ways.
One of the positive lessons learned was the need to treat each other with love and to refrain from dispensing abuse to their fellow men.

36

Monday came and the Kennedys had made all the preparations to have the chicken order delivered. Kenneth had already loaded the merchandise into the truck and was about to depart. Now with that out of the way, the main focus was now on the funeral.

Jeremiah had already made most of the preparations for the Wake and the funeral. There were nothing else left to do but wait on the dates. They expected a very large turnout for both events as the family was a prominent one, both inside and outside of the district.

They supplied chicken and eggs to most of the wholesales and meat shops within the parish. Kenneth is deeply involved in the development of soccer in the parish as an administrator in the Manchester Football Association. (MFA). Both he and his deceased brother were both active community persons in the recent past. Kenny was a master in the art of event planning, and used to organize community excursions in and around the parish of Manchester.

Now unlike the Dead Yard activities which tend to involve mostly residents of the district, the Wake usually attracts a large contingent of friends, family and business associates from outside of the district.

Kenneth, and more so Jeremiah, are quite verse with situations like these, and are well aware of the expectations. They have already cleared two acres of land which adjoins their home and rented additional tents, tables and chairs to facilitate the guests.

It was now the day of the Wake and activities at the Kennedys were fever pitch. Men were seen erecting tents; others were gathering wood for fuel to cook what is expected to be a grand feast. There were volunteer workers everywhere, working under the instruction of Jeremiah Kennedy. Danny Peart was setting up his BBQ grill, while his assistant sterilized three large aluminum pots which would be used for preparing the curry goat and white rice.

People started to make their way to the Wake much earlier than expected.

Vehicle operators were already beginning to find parking space a scarcity. After several hours, the yard and surrounding environs were swollen with people from all over. The police contingent was well pronounced, so were members of the business community and the Manchester Football Association.

The hired band played up a storm much to the delight of the crowd, who sang and danced to their every beat. The Wake was so successful that many of the attendants were still there to meet the morning sun.

The festive mood of the residents and other attendants at the Wake was replaced with sorrow at the funeral service. The service was officiated by three pastors including Freddy and went on for hours. The body was buried at the family plot just behind the Kennedy's home.

There was a sense of peace and tranquility across the district amidst the recent sorrows. Fear had disappeared, and the resolve of the people of this safe and peaceful district was strengthened. There were noticeable changes in attitude among the residents especially in the teenagers.

They were more respectful to each other and seemed to have developed better social interactions. But every now and then just to be sure, Mally and Freddy would look to make sure no new Kasha trees were growing close to any of the grave sites.

The end

Printed in Great Britain
by Amazon

41906367R00068